'Afraid you'll lose your reputation?' asked Josh.

'Of course *I* don't mind,' Phoebe said, 'but I thought you might.'

'Why, for heaven's sake? It's not criminal to hold a woman's hand. Or is that classed as sexual harrassment these days?'

Phoebe shook her head. 'No, of course not, but it's going to cause quite a stir for *you* to be seen holding hands with me. It's just something that *you*, as the boss, never do. You don't hold hands and you don't date women.'

Margaret O'Neill started scribbling at four and began nursing at twenty. She contracted TB and, when recovered, did her British Tuberculosis Association nursing training before general training at the Royal Portsmouth Hospital. She married, had two children, and with her late husband she owned and managed several nursing homes. Now retired and living in Sussex, she still has many nursing contacts. Her husband would have been delighted to see her books in print.

Recent titles by the same author:

THE GENEROUS HEART

MORE THAN SKIN-DEEP

BY

MARGARET O'NEILL

MILLS & BOON®

First published in Great Britain 1996
Large Print edition 1997
Harlequin Mills & Boon Limited,
Eton House, 18-24 Paradise Road, Richmond,
Surrey TW9 1SR

© Margaret O'Neill 1996

ISBN 0 263 15006 2

Set in Times by
Rowland Phototypesetting Limited
Bury St Edmunds, Suffolk

17-9705-50617-16-17

Printed and bound in Great Britain by
The Ipswich Book Company Limited, Ipswich

CHAPTER ONE

THE storm broke as the column of cars was peeling off the bypass just south of the county town of Heresham. Phoebe winced momentarily as a flash of lightning lit up the purple sky, almost blinding her. It was followed within moments by a great crash of thunder overhead.

Then came the rain. Huge, penny-sized drops of water hit the dusty road in front of her, bouncing off the dry surface and smashing into the windscreen of her tough little VW beetle. It was as dark as dusk. She put on the headlights and slowed down almost to walking pace, peering through the streaming glass to see what was ahead. The temperature, minutes before hot and humid, dropped dramatically.

The column crawled along the long straight of the Heresham Road as it approached the crossroads of a small Sussex village. In her rear mirror Phoebe could see the car behind her, a large green estate, weaving back and forth seeking a way round the slow-moving line of traffic.

The driver must be mad, she thought as it suddenly pulled out of line to overtake the vehicles ahead.

Simultaneously a car coming from the opposite direction materialised out of nowhere through the heavy downpour, lights blazing as it overtook the steady line of vehicles ahead of it. Both overtaking cars were on the crown of the road with no room to manoeuvre. It was madness. A head-on collision was inevitable.

Briefly distracted by the two vehicles tearing towards each other, Phoebe suddenly became aware that she was drawing dangerously near to the car in front of her, which had almost come to a halt. The car behind was fast closing the gap between them. She couldn't stop. Wet road, don't jam on brakes, might skid, instinct warned her. She held her breath. Her mind raced. What must she do? Switch on hazard lights—pull left onto the grass verge. She slewed round and stopped almost at right angles to the road, the nose of her car just touching the hedge that bordered the verge. The car behind her was within inches of her tail.

Stationary at an angle with the line of cars obscuring her vision, she couldn't see what was happening further along the road but moments after she stopped she heard the bang, the shattering of glass and the grinding, tearing sound of metal meeting metal as the two overtaking cars crashed into each other.

For a moment she was too dazed to move, her mind a blank. Then, suddenly and automatically, she began to function; began to think. There would be injured people—they would need help. A rush of adrenaline galvanised her into action. She must go and see what she could do. She stumbled out of the car and started to run past the halted row of vehicles towards the tangled mess of wreckage that lay ahead in the centre of the road.

Other people were getting out of their cars, most of them just standing and staring though one or two were moving cautiously forward towards the scene of the crash.

Phoebe, heart pumping madly, rushed past them.

A man tried to stop her. 'Don't go any nearer,' he said, grabbing her arm. 'It might be messy. . .'

Phoebe shook herself free. 'But I must,' she muttered, 'I'm a nurse.'

She pelted the last few yards through the pouring rain. She was drenched. Her bobbed, mahogany-brown hair was plastered against her scalp; her long lashes were beaded with drops.

Breathless, she reached the scene of the accident. A handful of people hovered uncertainly a few feet from the two smashed vehicles, mumbling amongst themselves and staring at the contorted mess in the middle of the road, obviously too shocked to do anything.

Phoebe knew that she must act—say something, get these people to rally round and do something constructive.

She was about to move forward and speak when a striking giant of a man, with thick, tawny blond hair and neatly cropped beard, strode up to the ring of spectators. He was well over six feet tall with massively broad shoulders matching his height. He was carrying a large briefcase.

'Let me through,' he said brusquely. 'I'm a doctor.'

The small group parted with a concerted murmur of relief, immediately recognising someone who would take charge.

Phoebe stepped in front of him. 'And I'm a nurse,' she said quickly, pushing down a moment of panic, feeling small and inadequate in spite of her five feet seven inches as she stared up at this large, assertive, bearded man. 'What can I do to help?'

A pair of cold, piercing blue eyes swept swiftly over her.

'Trained?' he snapped.

'Yes.'

'Done any casualty work?'

'Yes.'

'Right. You cope with the people in the estate car, assess them and do what you can. I'll check this one.' He indicated the low-slung, racy-looking sports model, its engine jammed like a concertina against the front and almost under the larger vehicle. The fractured windscreen bulged ominously outwards as if something hard and heavy had been thrust against it from within.

'OK,' replied Phoebe, praying that she would be able to 'cope', as he put it. She shivered with a mixture of wetness, cold and fear, aware that her thin silk shirt was clinging to her like a second skin.

The doctor dismissed her with a nod and turned to the group of still shocked bystanders, rattling off a list of instructions. 'Somebody call for police and ambulance and check that the people in the other cars nearby are all right. Some of them may have whiplash injuries if they stopped suddenly. Keep them immobile. And keep the centre of the road clear for access. Don't let any other idiot try to get past the parked cars.'

'OK, will do,' somebody said, and the small crowd began to disperse to do the doctor's bidding.

As he was speaking Phoebe, quaking inwardly and dreading what she would find, approached the nearside of the estate car. The laminated windscreen was a mosaic of cracks but, by some quirk of fate, the side window of toughened glass was miraculously intact. She peered through the steamy glass. There was no one in the front passenger seat but there were two small shadowy shapes in the back seat.

Children! She hadn't expected children.

No sound came from within the vehicle.

Her heart in her mouth, she opened the near-side door and slid into the seat beside the driver. She turned and quickly surveyed the children, her mind racing as she weighed up the situation. Who should she attend to first—the driver or the children? It was a big car. The rear seat was well away from the point of impact. At a quick glance the two small passengers appeared to be uninjured, still secured by their seat belts— though the younger one had slipped a little and was partly off her seat. They stared at her with wide eyes.

Phoebe smiled at them. 'Hello, girls,' she said softly. 'You've had an accident. You've bumped into another car but it's all over now; you're quite safe. Do you understand?'

They both nodded.

The older girl whispered, 'Is Mummy all right? She hasn't said anything. Is she hurt?'

Phoebe said. 'I'm going to look at her now.' She tried to sound confident and reassuring. 'She's had a nasty bump but I'm a nurse so I can help her.'

She turned to the driver. The young mother was held in place by her seat belt. Her back and neck were rigid. Whiplash? Blood was streaming from her nose and there was a large graze on her forehead and blood on the steering-wheel. She must have jerked forward and then backward on impact and banged her face. Her nose might be broken or just bruised.

Her right knee was jammed at an awkward angle against the dashboard and blood was oozing steadily through her torn jeans, from which a sliver of pale bone protruded, the ominous sign of an open fracture. Her hands were still clamped tightly on the steering-wheel, white to the knuckles. She was staring straight ahead of her. Was she dazed or unconscious or. . .?

Phoebe leaned over and felt at the woman's wrist for her radial pulse. A wave of relief washed over her. There was a pulse. It was fast but reasonably strong and regular so hopefully there was no internal bleeding.

As Phoebe touched her she began to stir and mumbled, 'Children in back.'

'They're all right,' said Phoebe. 'They're not hurt.'

The smaller of the two girls started to cry.

The woman tried to turn but whimpered with pain. 'I'm here, darling,' she murmured. 'Mummy's here.' Then she seemed to lapse into unconsciousness.

Phoebe felt helpless. She knew that she couldn't do much for the woman or the children except reassure them. She found a box of tissues in the door pocket and took a handful out and mopped at the bleeding nose. Ideally she should have tipped the patient's face forward to make sure that the airways remained clear but she dared not do this if there was a whiplash injury to the neck.

Both conditions were dicey—the risk of a broken neck if it was moved suddenly or lack of oxygen if the airways congested. But she seemed to be breathing all right at the moment and the bleeding might stop soon. Better protect the injured neck. Perhaps she should press the soft nostrils together to stem the bleeding, or would that make matters worse if there was a nasal fracture?

Feeling slightly panicky, so unlike her usual calm self, Phoebe wished the doctor was available to give advice.

At that moment the door beside her was opened a few inches and the doctor's coldly handsome face appeared mistily through the driving rain.

She said in a relieved voice, 'Oh you're here. You were quick. Is the other driver all right?'

He shook his head. 'No,' he said, in a low, expressionless voice, 'he's dead. Young bloke. No seat belt. Windscreen job.'

'Oh, no.' Her voice shook. A windscreen injury was the worst—she'd seen them in Casualty with unrecognisable, pulped faces.

'Bloody waste,' the doctor muttered ferociously but, though he sounded angry, his face remained inscrutable.

His cool, professional gaze swept dispassionately round the car, taking in the woman at the wheel and the wide-eyed little girls in the back seat. 'Now, what about this lot? The children don't look too bad, though they must be badly shaken. But the driver, how is she? Fill me in so that I know where to start.' He spoke rapidly but evenly, neither his voice nor his face giving anything away.

He doesn't seem to feel a thing, Phoebe thought, but she was grateful for his detached, authoritative manner and told him what she could, quietly and succinctly.

'She appears to be semi-conscious at the moment, though she spoke just now. Pulse fast but good volume. Nose probably broken. Looks as if there might be a whiplash injury to neck. Right leg fractured just below knee and wedged at odd angle against dashboard. I can't get at it from here but I can see a sliver of bone showing, probably tibia. Haven't had time to look at the children properly but, as you can see, they don't look physically injured, though they are shocked and frightened.'

He nodded. 'Right. I'll work from the other side so that I can see to that leg. You'd better take a closer look at the children and then give me a hand as soon as you can.'

The doctor disappeared round the side of the vehicle and Phoebe clambered into the back of the car.

It didn't take her long to do what she could for the two little girls. Carefully she lifted the younger one who had slipped partly through her belt back onto the seat, talking quietly to her all the time. She confirmed that neither she nor her sister appeared to be physically injured but the older one who had spoken to her earlier was now staring vacantly into space. They needed warmth and reassurance. She found cardigans crumpled on the seat beside them and wrapped them round their shoulders.

In answer to Phoebe's question, the little one gulped out that her name was Lucy and her sister's name was Kate. Phoebe turned her attention to the older girl, who looked at her with blank eyes.

Phoebe took her cold, clammy hands in hers and massaged them as she spoke to her gently. 'Kate, speak to me again. My name's Phoebe. It's all over now. You've had a little accident but you're all right and so is Lucy.' Gently she stroked the girl's cheeks. 'And your mother's going to be all right. A doctor is with her right now. She's injured but not too badly. Come on, Kate, Lucy needs you.'

Kate blinked and focussed on Phoebe. 'Mummy's not dead,' she whispered.

'No.'

Large tears rolled down the child's cheeks. 'I thought she might be. She said she wanted to die because Daddy had left us.'

Phoebe felt her heart contract with pity. 'Well, she hasn't died, love. Now listen, Kate, I'm going to help the doctor with your mother. Put your arm round Lucy and cuddle her. She's too little to understand what's happened. You must look after her for the moment. And you can do something for me—you can tell me what Mummy's name is so that I can talk to her.'

'Will she hear you?'

'I hope so.'

'Her name's Jane. Daddy used to call her "plain Jane" when he was cross but she isn't—she's pretty.' Kate's voice wobbled and tears welled up again in her eyes.

'Yes, she is pretty,' said Phoebe, glad that the child couldn't see the bloody, swollen nose and suffused, rapidly bruising flesh around her mother's eyes.

With the girls safely huddled together, Phoebe moved to the front of the car. The doctor was bent over the moaning, semi-conscious woman, examining her eyes with an ophthalmo-scope. His large medical case lay open on the passenger seat.

Phoebe lifted the open case and slid into the seat, nursing the case on her lap. 'I've done what I can back there,' she said. 'What can I do to help you?'

'Draw up two ml of pethidine for me to give intramuscularly,' he said curtly, without looking at her. 'This poor woman must be in agony with her shattered knee joint and shin—she needs a strong painkiller. I guess she's busted her patella and fractured her tib and fib.' He finished examining the woman's eyes.

'But at least she is only mildly concussed. There's no obvious sign of a skull fracture and her pupils are equal, though, of course, she's going to need an X-ray to confirm.'

It was on the tip of Phoebe's tongue to say that she was qualified and quite capable of giving the injection but she remained silent. Perhaps he wanted to give the injection himself, just to feel that he was doing something constructive, or perhaps he didn't trust her to give it.

She found the ampoule of pethidine in the well-stocked case, broke open a sterile syringe and drew up the powerful painkiller and handed it, with an antiseptic gauze swab, to the doctor. The injured woman was wearing a sleeveless vest and he was able to give the injection into the firm muscle of her upper arm without difficulty.

Although he was crouching in an awkward position with his back exposed to the pouring rain, his large, well-kept hands were rock steady and he talked to his patient in low but distinct tones as he slid the needle smoothly into her skin, explaining what he was doing even though he couldn't be sure that she could hear him.

Well, he might be chauvinistic and autocratic

in some respects, thought Phoebe as he handed her the empty syringe to dispose of in the specially marked container in his case, but his manner with his patient was first class.

She watched him as he crouched there, taking the woman's pulse and talking to her softly. He asked her her name but she only moaned and fluttered her eyelids restlessly. Phoebe knew that he was hoping for a response to confirm that she could hear and understand him. But when, after a moment, she didn't respond, Phoebe said quietly, 'It's Jane. I asked the girls.'

He glanced across at her and nodded, his spectacularly dark blue eyes meeting hers for an instant. 'Thanks. That was sensible of you,' he murmured tersely. 'It makes communication easier.'

A peculiar tremor passed through her as their eyes met. His look was strong and compelling, fierce and commanding. Inexplicably, she was glad that she had pleased him. It was a strange thought to have under the circumstances and was over in a flash but she felt a residual glow of satisfaction at his mild praise.

They both turned their attention back to the injured driver. There was now only a small trickle of blood coming from her nose. The doctor wiped it away with a tissue.

'Jane,' he said distinctly, speaking close to her ear, 'you've hurt your leg badly and have broken some bones but the injection that I've just given you should ease the pain a little. Now I'm going to put something over the wound in your leg to keep it clean and I'll have to cut your jeans away so that I can get to it. That's all I can do till the ambulance gets here. Do you understand?'

Jane moaned and muttered incoherently.

Anticipating his needs while he was speaking, Phoebe found and handed him scissors from his case. Then she unearthed a pack of sterile dressings and a wide bandage and had them at the ready when he had finished cutting away the material. There was nothing more that she could do for the moment.

She watched as with sure fingers he gently eased the injured knee away from the dashboard sufficiently to secure a dressing over the open wound.

He looked up at her from his crouching position. 'Can't do anything else,' he said flatly. 'Might do more harm than good. Let's pray that the ambulance gets here soon.'

As if in answer to his prayer they heard the wail of both police and ambulance sirens in the distance and within seconds several vehicles arrived. Two ambulances and three police cars.

Everything seemed to happen very fast after that.

Even the weather co-operated with the arrival of the emergency services. It stopped raining as abruptly as it had begun, though thunder continued to rumble around the distant horizon. Within minutes the clouds parted and the sun suddenly blazed out.

Quickly and competently the paramedics and a casualty officer took over from Phoebe and the doctor. Briefly the two doctors conferred together. The two small girls were taken to one of the ambulances by a cheerful driver and a smiling policewoman, who spoke reassuringly to them. And shortly afterwards their mother was expertly manoeuvred onto a stretcher and transferred to the ambulance by the medical team.

The second ambulance took away the dead driver of the sports car.

And suddenly, following the bustling noise

and activity, there was nothing for Phoebe and the doctor to do except wait to be questioned by the police, as they had been requested.

Silently, side by side, they stood on the grass verge watching the ambulances, sirens wailing, speed away. Now that their part in the drama had ended it seemed that they had nothing to say to each other. The doctor looked remote and unapproachable, Phoebe thought, and, as if to emphasise this, he half turned away from her and stared into the distance. He obviously had no intention of even trying to make conversation.

Oh, well, be like that, she thought crossly, and turned to watch the police as they started to move the traffic on until the road was almost clear of parked vehicles and a steady stream of traffic moved past. Only half a dozen cars remained in the immediate vicinity of the accident, besides the tangled wreckage of the two cars involved.

Way up the road, all by itself, Phoebe could see her little yellow beetle with its nose in the hedge. And, facing north, a long way down the road on the opposite side stood an isolated, dark blue, sleek-looking car, which she guessed belonged to the doctor.

Policemen were taking statements from the occupants of the nearby cars who had seen the accident at close range and then one of the officers detached himself from the group and moved across to where Phoebe and the doctor were standing on the grass verge.

'Sorry to keep you waiting,' he said politely. 'I have to ask a few questions about what you found when you arrived at the scene of the accident.'

Had either of the drivers smelt of alcohol? he wanted to know.

'No,' said Phoebe, 'the driver of the estate car didn't.'

'Yes,' said the doctor in a clipped, hard voice, 'the driver of the sports car did and the fool hadn't been wearing a seat belt either.'

'Do you think he was over the limit?' asked the officer.

'I've no idea,' said the doctor curtly.

'Could either of the drivers have had a heart attack or a fit or anything that might have contributed towards the accident?'

'That's something that only further examination or an autopsy will reveal,' said the doctor. 'There was nothing about the woman to indicate that there was anything wrong with her, other than the injuries that she sustained but I was only able to examine her superficially.'

His deep, measured tones suddenly gave way to pent-up anger. 'How could a mother drive like a maniac with her children on board? How *could* she? She might have killed those two little girls. Some females,' he said savagely, 'shouldn't be allowed behind the wheel of a car.' He frowned and stared at Phoebe with hard, blank eyes, as if he wasn't really seeing her and, fleetingly, an expression of what she thought was pain flitted across his face.

How incredible that he should react so angrily, Phoebe thought. He had seemed too calm and remotely professional to give way to his feelings. And why vent his wrath on the woman, on all women, as he'd seemed to do? The man in this case had been equally culpable—more culpable, in fact, if he'd been drinking. It just wasn't fair. He obviously had a thing about women and women drivers in particular. Of all the arrogant, chauvinistic men, he really was the end. She would have liked to challenge him but it was not the time or place.

The officer made no comment on what the doctor had said but went on to ask them if they could tell him anything about the crash itself but they were unable to help. Neither of them had been very near at the moment of impact though they had seen the cars rushing toward each other.

'And was the estate car involved in the accident behind you in the line of traffic?' the officer asked Phoebe.

'Yes, immediately behind me,' she confirmed.

'And that is your car parked on the grass verge up there?' He pointed to her lonely beetle.

'Yes, I swerved to avoid bumping into the car in front or being hit by the vehicle behind when the traffic began to close up after the car that was involved in the crash overtook me.'

'Hmm,' said the officer, frowning. 'You weren't going too fast in these conditions?'

'Certainly not. I was barely crawling but the car in front of me almost stopped. I think the driver was surprised by the estate car overtaking him,' she said, trying to squash a little spurt of anger and keep her voice level, very conscious of the bearded doctor beside her and his opinion of women drivers. 'Look here, you aren't suggesting that I had anything to do with the accident, are you?'

The officer shook his head. 'No,' he said evenly. 'I just wanted to know if you started swerving before the estate car overtook you.'

'Well, I didn't,' Phoebe said firmly. 'Now, please may I go? I have an appointment to keep.'

'And I,' said the doctor abruptly. He took something from the breast pocket of his linen jacket and thrust it towards the policeman. 'Here's my card. You can contact me any time, officer, if you want further information.'

'Thank you, sir.' The man accepted the card and tucked it into his notebook.

To Phoebe's surprise the doctor turned to her and, with a glimmer of a smile which didn't quite reach his eyes, offered her a large hand. After a moment's hesitation she slipped her much smaller one into it. To her further surprise he pressed it gently and said firmly, 'Thank you, Nurse, for all your help. You were splendid. I couldn't have managed without you. Goodbye.' He released her hand, nodded to the policeman, turned on his heel and strode away toward his car, his broad shoulders and well-shaped head with its mane of tawny blond hair silhouetted against the brilliant sunshine.

A few minutes later he raised a hand in a farewell salute as he drove past in his sleek, dark blue Jaguar. The colour of his eyes, thought Phoebe inconsequentially as it sped northwards toward Heresham.

CHAPTER TWO

SHORTLY after the doctor had driven away Phoebe, having given her name and address to the police, was free to continue her interrupted journey.

Before getting the beetle back on the road she spent a few minutes repairing her ravaged make-up and running a comb through her short, thick mop of mahogany-brown hair. Her hand, she noticed with annoyance, was slightly unsteady and she still felt somewhat shaken by all that had happened. She peered in the mirror and saw that, thanks to standing in the hot sunshine after the rain had stopped, both her hair and her thin silk shirt had almost dried out. At least by the time she arrived at her destination she shouldn't look too scruffy to present herself for her new job.

Consulting her map, she continued to drive south but after a few miles she left the main highway to drive along a narrow road skirting the gentle undulations of the south downs.

She drove carefully, her mind still full of the accident, the injured young mother and the two little girls. What would happen to them? Would the police contact her estranged husband? Would the accident bring them together?

Phoebe sighed—that was something she would never know. The accident and all that went with it was over and done with. A tragic, closed episode. She had played her part to the best of her ability and must now put it out of her mind and forget it.

A tractor pulled out of a farm gate ahead of her and she had to slow to a crawl, giving her more time to think.

But she couldn't forget the accident; it continued to haunt her. She wondered about the dead driver of the sports car, with his smashed face and other horrific injuries—typical of 'a windscreen job'! He must have a partner or parents who would be heartbroken by his death.

What a waste of a young life—even the cool, correct doctor had been moved to anger by it. For a moment the glacial blue eyes had reflected that anger as, with rain beading his tawny hair and close-cut beard, he had crouched by the estate car and told her that the man was dead.

A strange man, the doctor. Arrogant and contemptuous of women drivers yet so tender and compassionate when dealing with the injured woman. Formidably good-looking, with his chiselled cheek-bones, high bridged nose and brilliant blue eyes. And those shoulders were quite something. Pity about the beard.

Though some women would like it; would consider that it made him sexy, in spite of his aloofness. No doubt he'd got a timid, adoring wife somewhere who thought so. She would be chained to the kitchen sink, where he thought all women belonged, caring for a houseful of beautiful children with fair hair and vivid blue eyes, all ready to adore him too.

Impatiently she shook her head to dispel the vivid picture of the doctor which, for some unaccountable reason, had lodged in her head. 'What the hell does it matter what the wretched man's like or whether he's married or not?' she muttered through gritted teeth. 'I'm never going to see him again, which is just as well because I hate men with beards—they can't be trusted.'

Common sense told her that she was being irrational. Just because Neil, black-bearded and good-looking in a dark, rather saturnine fashion, had turned out to be weak, unreliable and untrustworthy there was no reason to assume that all bearded men were the same. Anyway, there were plenty of clean-shaven men who behaved just as badly. It was a silly, ridiculous notion. Neil would have been Neil, beard or no beard.

Suppressing a wave of sadness and with a snort of disgust at the way her thoughts were taking her, she turned her attention back to the road. It was best not to think of what might have been: she and Neil had parted and that was that. She was now going to look forward to the future and enjoy life. She would put the past behind her; take no emotional baggage with her to Richmond Place. She wouldn't mention the past to anyone.

From now she would start with a clean slate.

There was a turning just ahead of her— Church Lane, leading to Pheasant's Green and ultimately to Richmond Place and her new job.

She turned into the twisting, leafy lane. The rain-fresh, green hedges on either side were starred with the flat faces of pale pink blossoming dog-roses and the grass verges were thick with white lacy fronds of cow parsley, with a spattering of scarlet poppies in between.

The lane widened, branched to right and left and suddenly she was there at Pheasant's Green. It was a pretty village full of thatched and tile-hung cottages gathered round a carefully tended oval of grass with a wooden pavilion at one end. She drove up one side of the green, getting her bearings. There was a squat-towered medieval church at one corner, an ancient pub at another and halfway round the green a small general shop and post office. It was idyllic. Picture postcard perfect.

Phoebe sighed with pleasure. It was late May, high summer in the heart of the English countryside where she was going to work and live for the next few weeks or possibly months. Surely if anything was going to heal the trauma caused by her parting from Neil it was here, in rural Sussex, doing an interesting, worthwhile job in delightful surroundings.

A pair of massive brick pillars stood at the north end of the green, each topped by a proud-faced stone lion. On one pillar an elegant signboard in black and gold announced that this was: RICHMOND PLACE, REGISTERED REHABILI-TATION, CONVALESCENT AND HOLIDAY HOME.

A driveway opened out between stately wrought-iron gates, laid back against the massive brick pillars and curved gently upwards between acres of rolling pasture interspersed with clusters of oak, beech and lime trees.

The house was just visible from a distance across the park. A large sprawling mass of rose-pink brickwork under a tiled roof, with tall, elegant chimneys and dozens of windows glinting in the sunlight.

Crossing a hump back bridge over a small, fast-running stream, she found herself within a few hundred yards of the house. Parkland and pasture gave way to crowded, colourful herbaceous borders full of massed flowers, a crescent of smoothly mown lawn and a large, circular sweep of golden gravel where several cars were parked beneath the trees that bordered it on one side.

Everything was very still. The house and grounds slumbered in the hot afternoon sunshine.

She parked beneath the spreading branches of a massive linden tree, which cast some welcome shade.

For a moment she sat savouring the peace

and quiet that surrounded her, broken only by the gentle hum of insects hovering amongst the lime-green leaves above.

Well, here it was—Richmond Place, an Elizabethan manor house at its best; stately, yet homely and welcoming. But what would it be like to live and work in? How would she fit in with the staff and patients in this unique set-up which seemed to be part hospital, part luxury hotel?

Her stomach contracted. This was her first agency job; her first experience of working outside of a hospital proper away from friends she had worked with for years. It was a shattering thought. She took a deep breath, squared her shoulders and heaved her luggage from the back seat of the beetle.

'Well, it's no good getting cold feet now, Palmer,' she muttered as she crunched across the gravel to the portico entrance. 'Too late to have second thoughts. Once more into the breach, and all that.'

Busy with bees, sweet-scented honeysuckle and dark purple wistaria wreathed the pillars of the portico and the balcony above it. A massive iron-studded oak door stood wide open and

Phoebe stepped from the scorching hot sunshine into the large, cool entrance hall.

The hall was empty. She stood just inside the doorway and gazed round her.

It was dim after the brilliance outside but a gleaming silver bowl, filled with fragrant, multi-coloured sweet peas, glowed on an old, well-polished refectory table gracing the centre of the hall. And beneath high windows there were side tables and more flowers. And at one end of the hall was an impressive marble fireplace with an ornate brass fender, where a magnificent display of tall, royal blue delphiniums, dusky pink lupins and spikes of lavender filled the empty grate.

Beside the fireplace a gracious staircase, built of some pale, golden wood that she didn't recognise, curved up to a balcony that encircled the hall.

At the other end of the room a crescent-shaped reception desk in the same pale wood as the staircase occupied one corner and, beside it, a wide archway led into an equally wide corridor.

Phoebe crossed to the desk and pressed the old-fashioned brass bell that stood on the counter. A murmur of voices coming from behind a half-open door marked OFFICE ceased and, in answer to the bell, a plump, pretty, middle-aged woman with fair curly hair emerged from the inner room.

She gave Phoebe a nice smile. 'Well, hello,' she said cheerfully. 'Sorry to keep you waiting.'

'You haven't,' said Phoebe, returning her smile. 'I've only just arrived. I'm—'

'Let me guess,' the woman interrupted, her smile widening. 'You're the new replacement nurse we've been expecting.' Phoebe nodded. 'Lovely to see you. Welcome to Richmond Place. I'm Kathy Martin, senior receptionist.'

Phoebe shook the plump hand held out to her. 'And I'm Phoebe Palmer,' she said. 'How nice to have such a warm welcome.'

'Well, there's someone who'll give you an even warmer one,' said Kathy. 'She's the other resident full-time nurse on the medical team and has been holding the fort on her own for the last few days so you can imagine how pleased she'll be to see you; and she's right here.' She called over her shoulder, 'Maeve, show yourself; come and see who's arrived.'

A tall, well-built, attractive young woman,

with bright green eyes and a mop of fiery red hair, emerged from the office. She stopped dead when she saw Phoebe and gave a little shriek. 'By all the saints, it's Phoebe Palmer.' She rushed round the counter and gave Phoebe a bear hug.

Phoebe exclaimed in an astonished voice, 'Maeve, Maeve Connelly!'

Kathy beamed at them both. 'How super,' she said. 'You know each other.'

'We trained at the same hospital yonks ago,' said Maeve.

'When we were young and innocent and full of plans for the future and all life was before us,' said Phoebe with a laugh.

'Well, I don't know about the innocent bit but you're not exactly *old* now,' said Kathy drily. 'I can give you a good few years and I still feel that I've a bit of life left in me.' She gave Maeve a push. 'Go on, take Phoebe up to her room and then give her a tour round. I'll bleep you if you're needed.'

For Phoebe the next hour sped past as Maeve whisked her round on a whirlwind tour of the house, pouring out information interspersed with reminiscences of the old days, with lots of:

'Do you remember when. . .?' and: 'Whatever happened to old. . .?'

They started their tour on the second floor, where the live-in staff were accommodated. An old-fashioned lift, with mirrored walls and gold plaster mouldings, swished them smoothly upwards.

The lift stopped at the end of a wide corridor with white-painted doors on one side. On the opposite side sunshine streamed in through open windows onto the polished floor.

Near the lift was a door marked: PRIVATE. 'Lady Richmond's apartment,' Maeve explained. 'Elegant, stately rooms—like the old lady herself. She's a grand old thing but very friendly. She invites us in for drinks or coffee from time to time.'

'And who is Lady Richmond?' Phoebe asked.

'She owns the home. Well, she and her grand-son do. It's been in their family since for ever. Without the Richmonds this place wouldn't exist. They're pretty special. You'll see what I mean when you get to know them.'

They walked past several closed doors to a door facing down the hall.

'And this,' said Maeve, opening the door with

a flourish, 'is our utility room, with all mod cons.' It was beautifully equipped with a microwave oven, fridge, toaster and hot plate, washing machine, tumbler drier and sink unit. There was a red and white tiled floor, with check curtains at the window to match, an electric kettle and steam iron and a multiplicity of power points, working surfaces and cupboards.

Phoebe was impressed. 'Hey, this is brilliant,' she said.

'Isn't it just?' said Maeve, beaming at her, clearly pleased by her reaction. 'We generally eat in the dining-room but, as you can see, everything's laid on for us to do for ourselves if we want to. And now come and look at your room, just across here, and mine's next to yours.'

Phoebe's room was delightful. Large, light and airy, with chintz curtains at the casement windows that looked out over the rolling parkland and a chintz coverlet on the bed to match. A pale, polished wood desk and chair stood beneath the window and a comfortable-looking easy chair against one wall. A door beside it led into a minute shower room with a loo and washbasin.

Phoebe was even more impressed. 'My goodness, they do do you well here,' she said to Maeve.

Her friend said with proprietorial pride, 'Oh, it's a grand place to work. Old Lady Richmond converted the house to a rehabilitation and holiday home just after the war and is very hot on looking after the staff as well as the residents.'

'Is she still active in the home?'

Maeve laughed. 'Not exactly. She's ninety plus, white hair, regal, walks with sticks. She puts in an appearance most days but leaves the running of the place to her grandson, Josh. He's a doctor, our boss. A great guy to work for, though his manner's a bit offish at first until he gets to know you. He gives the impression of being remote but he's not really.' She rolled her eyes theatrically.

'He's stunning, actually. Georgeous, sexy. We'd all give our eye teeth to date him but he just isn't interested in women. The grapevine has it that he had an accident a few years ago and his fiancée jilted him, leaving him poleaxed. But that's only rumour—even the staff who were here at the time don't know much.

He's out at the moment but you'll meet him later.'

After Phoebe had deposited her luggage, tidied up and had a welcome cup of tea they made their way to the floor below. Here, Maeve explained as they walked along the wide, richly carpeted corridor, residents were accomodated in single or double rooms.

There was no one about. The doors on either side of the corridor were firmly shut.

'It's so quiet,' said Phoebe. 'Not a bit like a hospital.'

'That's because it isn't one,' replied Maeve. 'Residents come and go as they please. But most of them on this floor are either convalescent and rest in the afternoon or are on holiday and out and about. Everyone is encouraged to lead a normal life where possible, though some of them are advised not to go far afield without an escort.'

'Who does the escorting?'

'Generally the care assistants. Some of them live in and others come up from the village. You'll be meeting them later. They're a nice bunch. They help people to bed if needed, take round night drinks and so on and generally assist the nurses and other qualified staff—physios, occupational and massage therapists. One way and another there's quite an army of helpers.'

'Then what do we do, for heaven's sake, just trip around and try to look busy?'

'Oh, don't worry, we're busy enough— assisting in the surgery and dispensary and with admission examinations; seeing to injections, wound care, medicine rounds and so on. And one of us is on call at night, though the actual staffing is done by the care assistants and auxiliaries. And, of course, we supervise generally and escort when necessary. There's plenty of nursing to do for the two of us, with help from the part-time registered nurses.

'But everything's orientated toward rehabilitation and getting people back to an active life, whether in wheelchairs or on their own two feet.'

'Does that mean that all the patients are referred from hospital?'

'Lord, no. Most are but many come from home for a holiday. Or, if they are severely disabled, they come to give their relatives a rest from looking after them. This especially applies to paraplegics and the chronically ill.'

'And how many residents are there?'

'Seventy when we're full and we nearly always are. Thirty up here and the rest down-stairs.'

The balcony overlooking Reception opened off the end of the first-floor corridor and, instead of taking the lift, they walked down the gracious staircase to the ground floor.

From the stairs they could see that the hall, which had been so quiet earlier, was now a hive of activity. There was a group of people milling round the reception desk, keeping Kathy busy. Two of them, a young woman and an elderly man, were in wheelchairs being pushed by car-ers but the third, a young man with one leg, was swinging confidently across the hall on elbow crutches.

'New admissions,' explained Maeve, 'from the Heresham General Hospital. They've all come for physio and general rehabilitation and trauma control. The care staff will settle them in their rooms and I'll see them later to collect a medical history. And tomorrow Josh will give them a complete physical and discuss their rehabilitation programmes.

'It might be a good idea if you assist him and find out what he's like to work with. Don't worry if he seems a bit distant at first. That's just his way with newcomers; he soon softens up.'

'I'm glad to hear it,' said Phoebe drily. 'Your Dr Richmond sounds rather formidable.'

Maeve laughed. 'He's not really. His bark's worse than his bite; he's really a very gentle guy. Now, let's finish looking around.'

The rest of the tour was fascinating for Phoebe as there was so much to see. Maeve took her round the four-bedded and double rooms on the ground floor and she met a couple of the residents.

There was a young woman, Paula Bryant, who smiled brightly and spoke cheerfully, though suffering from lumbosacral spasm—a painful condition of the spine. She was, for the moment, being treated by bed rest, muscle relaxants and analgesics. But later, Maeve said, she would receive gentle massage therapy to treat the soft tissues of the body; to soothe and relax and, hopefully, get her back on her feet. She would then probably move on to physiotherapy and more vigorous exercise.

In another four-bedded room a young man,

David Thorn, recently rendered paralysed from the waist downwards through a motorcycle accident, only nodded to Phoebe when she greeted him. He had been admitted from hospital the previous day and a physiotherapist, whom Maeve introduced as Jill Daly, and a carer, Phil Knight, were with him, encouraging him to do deep breathing and arm and shoulder exercises, but he was being rude and uncooperative.

'I don't want your bloody help,' he said as Maeve and Phoebe moved away from his bed. 'Just leave me alone. I can't walk and there's an end to it.'

'Oh, poor man, he seems to have given up. Will you ever be able to do anything for him?' Phoebe asked.

'Oh, yes, almost certainly,' replied Maeve. 'Given time and with bags of patience and hard work and counselling. One day he'll somehow dredge up the courage to go on. And once he starts getting to know the other guys with similar disabilities he'll begin to make progress. That's the usual pattern.'

The other wards were empty. 'Most of them are in the activity centre at this time of day,' explained Maeve. 'That's where we're going next.'

A glass-roofed pergola, wreathed with rambling roses that were rich with early, velvety red blooms and heavy with scent, connected the main building to the activity centre, where she was introduced to more patients and staff.

The centre was magnificently equipped with a pool, a gymnasium, a bowling alley and club room; further buildings housed shooting and archery ranges. Nothing, it seemed, was too good for the residents of Richmond Place. It was run like a luxury hotel-cum-hospital and all due to the generosity of the Richmond family.

Phoebe and Maeve parted at five o'clock, Phoebe to unpack and settle in and Maeve to attend to her evening chores. They arranged to meet at half-past seven in the dining-room.

Phoebe unpacked slowly and thoughtfully, her mind a kaleidoscope of all that she had seen that afternoon. Richmond Place was certainly impressive. There was a 'feel' about it, an ambience, that was almost tangible. And nearly everyone she had met had been smiling and friendly. Obviously morale was high. It had been wonderful to see even the severely disabled moving effortlessly through the blue-green waters of the pool; or doing complicated exercises on the bars and equipment in the gym; or shooting with varying degrees of skill at the targets on the ranges.

It was astonishing to see how they had come to terms with their physical handicaps, over-coming seemingly improbable odds. It would be an entirely new experience for a nurse trained for acute medicine but the omens were good. With lovely surroundings and a happy staff, it ought to be a great place to work in.

But what of Dr Josh Richmond, her boss? Would he be friendly or difficult to get on with? He sounded a rather off-putting sort of charac-ter, though Maeve had defended him, saying that his bark was worse than his bite. She hoped it was—she hoped that she would be able to cope with him.

Normally she was a fighter and well able to hold her own but since her bust-up with Neil she'd felt vulnerable, unsure of herself. She was prepared to work hard—wanted to do so—but she needed a period of calm to reorientate herself.

Well, the doctor might be the one fly in the

ointment in the otherwise perfect setting of Richmond Place but she would learn to work with him.

On this resolve she finished her unpacking, had a shower and changed into a sleeveless, short, white cotton shift dress patterned all over with scarlet poppies—like the ones in Church Lane, she thought as she slipped her feet into white strappy sandals. She gave her bob of dark hair a quick brush, put on a touch of make up, sprayed herself with sandalwood perfume and let herself out of her room.

The hall was very quiet. Dust motes danced in the muted evening sunlight shining through the open, west-facing windows. It was all very peaceful.

As Phoebe started to cross the hall the door to Lady Richmond's apartment was partially opened.

Phoebe paused. Was she to meet that remarkable lady sooner than expected?

The door was opened wide and a shadowy figure stood silhouetted briefly in the doorway. But the silhouette was not of an elderly lady but that of a tall, broad-shouldered man.

He stepped out of the dimness of the recessed

doorway into the dusky sunlight, closing the door quietly behind him.

Phoebe froze, rooted to the spot as she stared across at the large, handsome man with the mane of tawny hair.

Her heart seemed to stand still for endless minutes. Then she said breathlessly, '*You*! Oh, no, *you*'re not Dr Richmond?'

The man inclined his head slightly. 'Oh, but I am.' He frowned and then recognition dawned. 'Good Lord,' he said in a faintly surprised voice. 'We meet again but this time under less traumatic circumstances and. . .' he paused, his lips twitched at the corners and he raised an expressive eyebrow '. . .you're looking rather drier this time, altogether less—well—wet!'

'You too,' said Phoebe, giving him the glimmer of a smile.

'How true, we were both rather like drowned rats this morning.'

Only this morning! Their tentative smiles disappeared and they stared silently at each other, remembering the accident in grim detail: the contused, bloodied face and bashed-in skull of the dead man, the semi-conscious woman's leg, contorted into an impossible angle with its gaping wound and ominous sliver of bone; the two small, terrified girls.

Josh broke the silence. He knew what she was thinking. He said quietly, 'Try not to dwell on it. Put it behind you. You did what you could at the time. We both did.'

'I wish we could have done more.'

'One always wishes that, Miss Palmer,' he said in a bitter, hard voice.

Surprised, Phoebe said, 'How on earth do you know my name? I haven't introduced myself.'

He shrugged and said drily, 'Not difficult. Simple deduction. Sherlock Holmes stuff. You've just come out of one of the staff bed-rooms; I know you're a nurse, and they told me in Reception that the agency nurse had arrived. Bingo, you had to be that nurse.'

He seemed unruffled by her arrival on his home patch and she was determined to match his calm. If he wasn't to be shaken by their unlikely meeting neither was she. She walked toward him and held out her hand. 'Of course, I see that it was obvious, Dr Richmond.'

He stepped forward and took her hand in his. 'Welcome to Richmond Place,' he said but though his voice was cool the pressure of his fingers seemed to Phoebe warm and reassuring. 'I'm sorry I wasn't here to meet you. Have you had a chance to look round?'

'Yes. Maeve Connelly gave me a conducted tour.'

He nodded. 'Good, I'm glad that you've met her. Maeve's a delightful, friendly young woman and a well-trained, dedicated and loyal nurse—just the sort of person we like to have here. We usually vet all our staff closely before employing them and never normally consider agency nurses but, because of the rather unusual circumstances, you slipped in under the net as it were. But having seen you in action, I'm sure you'll do well in a relief capacity.'

Clearly his reassuring handshake meant very little; he was obviously reserving judgement on her.

She swallowed a little spurt of anger. Did he have to be so damned arrogant, just as he had been at the accident?

She took several deep breaths and forced herself to stay calm. She would have liked to have told him where he could stuff his precious job but she needed it for both financial and personal reasons. And hard work was essential to get

Neil out of her system so that she could start to live again and Richmond Place was perfect for the purpose. Well, Maeve had warned her that he might be difficult initially; that she shouldn't be surprised by his manner.

After a moment, in a controlled, well-modulated voice, she said, 'Well, Dr Richmond, like Maeve I'm well-trained and loyal and have excellent references. In fact, she and I trained together and have known each other for years. . . And I'm sure she'd be willing to vouch for me,' she added with a touch of sarcasm.

He ignored the sarcasm. 'That's splendid,' he said in a cool voice. 'There's nothing like personal recommendation. I'm sure she will endorse the excellent verbal references given to me by the agency.' Whilst they were talking they had moved over to stand by the lift and he stretched out a hand and pressed the wall button. 'Presumably you are on the way down to the dining-room. . .' It was half a question, half a statement.

'Yes,' she said shortly.

'I hope you enjoy your meal.'

'Thank you.'

The lift whispered to a halt a moment later

and the doors opened. The doctor ushered her in and stepped in behind her. 'I'm going to the first floor,' he said, punching the appropriate button, 'to look in on a patient. I'll see you in the morning in my private office at eight-thirty sharp to discuss your duties and fill you in on anything that Maeve may have left out.'

'I'll be there, Dr Richmond, on the dot,' she said stiffly.

He nodded. The lift stopped smoothly. 'Goodnight,' he said, formally, as he stepped out. Then, to her utter astonishment, he turned and added softly, 'Sleep well, Phoebe, and don't worry about tomorrow. I'm sure you're going to fit in here at Richmond Place. You have the right. . .' he paused '. . .for want of a better word—aura.' His well-defined mouth curved into a gentle smile and his brilliant blue eyes reflected that smile, taking her completely by surprise. He was suddenly friendly; all arrogance had fled.

For a long moment she stared at his wide retreating back as he walked away and noted in a detached fashion that he was limping slightly. Her mind was in turmoil. What a man; what an enigma! How could he be brusque and almost rude one moment and so warm and friendly the next?

Well, Maeve had warned her that he was something of a dual personality and that behind the sometimes remote manner there lurked a kind and sensitive man and doctor; it seemed that she had been privileged to see both sides of his nature this evening. But what of tomorrow? What side of his intriguing nature would he show then?

She sighed and pressed the button for the ground floor. She would just have to wait and see.

CHAPTER THREE

THE next morning Phoebe woke early, having slept dreamlessly. She felt wonderfully refreshed. It was as if she had blindly obeyed Josh's instructions to sleep well; it was as if, in those few minutes when he had stepped out of the lift, he had hypnotised her into doing just that, she thought wryly. But that was too fanciful.

Her sound sleep was more likely due to a couple of glasses of the famous local cider and the relaxed evening she had spent with Maeve and some of the other staff at the Richmond Arms and, not least, to her long, eventful day.

The morning was full of birdsong and slanting sunshine and fresh country air, a fitting start to her first full day at Richmond Place. Feeling too wide awake and restless to stay in bed, she got up and padded across to the open window, perched herself on the wide sill and gazed out over the peaceful parkland where an ethereal golden mist hung above the grass. She could

55

see the stream sparkling in the sunlight, cows in a distant field and horses in a nearer paddock.

After the bustle and fumes and noise of London and her bitter, sad affair with Neil it seemed a quiet haven where she could come to rest and lick her wounds. A perfect bolt-hole.

But life wasn't like that, she reminded herself sharply, even at Richmond Place. It wasn't all pastoral peace but rather a place where the sick came to face up to sometimes seemingly impossible odds. It was not just a holiday hotel where people chose to come to enjoy themselves but an extension of hospital where the frail and often chronically ill, young and old, in various stages of hope or despair, were sent to rebuild their lives.

And she was there to help them do just that— to come to terms with pain and trauma. For many it was a stopover between hospital and home.

Her own emotional problems were as nothing by comparison and must be well and truly squashed. She must concentrate on being the dedicated nurse Josh Richmond would expect her to be.

Dr Richmond! Her heart did a curious little

flip at the thought of this enigmatic man who was her boss. Ultimately, she had him to answer to for, in spite of his totally unexpected, softened manner when they had parted last evening, she was aware that he would be watching her like a hawk to see that she maintained the high standards that he demanded where his patients were concerned. He would be tough and unforgiving if she failed and those brilliant blue eyes would turn to ice and annihilate her.

What made him tick? she wondered. What made him content to work in a small medical unit caring for a comparatively few traumatised patients needing long-term support, however worthwhile that might be, rather than in a high-powered department in one of the large teaching hospitals?

She judged him to be in his mid-thirties and Maeve had said that he was a super doctor. So what was he doing here when he could be well up the professional ladder as a senior registrar with a top surgical firm and the promise of a consultancy within his grasp?

It was easy to picture him as a surgeon. She recalled the long, lean, steady fingers that had tended Jane, the young mother injured in the accident. He had been every inch a surgeon then, exuding confidence, control and authority, though there had been a suppressed fury about him—a boiling anger at what had happened, especially the involvement of the two little girls.

'How could a mother drive like a maniac with her children on board?' he'd said through gritted teeth when the police officer had been questioning them. 'How *could* she?' And his eyes had turned to flint.

And how ferociously and chauvinistically he had condemned women drivers in general, as if all the accidents on all the roads were down to them.

Phoebe sighed. What a strange mixture the man was—alternately caustic and kind. Would she ever get to know him?

It was at that very moment that she saw him walking across the humpback bridge over the stream.

Even at this distance she could see that he was striding out confidently, not limping as he had been last night. His tall, broad frame was lit by the morning sun and his mane of tawny hair was glowing like a halo. No wonder most of the female staff fancied him. He was like a picture in a child's book of legends—god-like—an all-conquering, fearless pirate of a man on the deck of a Viking ship. It was a pity that he seemed to have a chip on his bshoulder. Pity about the beard, she thought inconsequentially; he would look even more handsome if he was clean shaven.

Suddenly she brought herself up with a jolt. What on earth was she thinking of? It mattered not one iota to her what he was like as a man or what he looked like: all she was concerned about was what he would be like to work with as a doctor, her employer; men as men she could do without. She snorted with derision at herself for daydreaming and putting on her dressing-gown, took herself off to the utility room to make tea.

At half-past eight on the dot, feeling surprisingly tense and nervous, like a raw student applying for a first job, she thought crossly, she knocked at the door of Josh's admin office on the ground floor.

'Come,' he called tersely.

Why was he so abrupt? Did it mean that he was in one of his icily polite moods? She suppressed a flutter in the region of her stomach and pushed open the door.

She had expected to find him seated at his desk but he was not. He was standing motionless, silhouetted against the bright window.

'Good morning,' said Phoebe brightly to his broad back.

'Shush,' he muttered in a low voice without turning. 'Come here; come and look at this.' He motioned her nearer. She moved across the room and stood beside him. 'Look,' he said softly, pointing into the garden, 'a family of foxes.'

There were four foxes on the lawn, a vixen and three cubs leaping and gambolling about on the dewy grass. They seemed unafraid, oblivious to the fact that they were near the house and were being watched. The sunlight glinted on their reddish brown fur, setting it on fire.

'Oh,' breathed Phoebe. 'Aren't they beautiful? I've never seen a real live fox before.'

'That's because you're a city girl,' said Josh, 'and wild things prefer the country. Though they are to be seen in the heart of London. When I was at the Central and had been on duty for God knows how many hours I saw a fox and a hare, of all elusive creatures, on the grubby strip of grass that passed for a garden.

'It was like something out of *Alice in Wonderland*—a fox and a hare a few yards from each other! There was something magic about it—very soothing, very therapeutic.' He looked down at her and grinned, raising a sardonic eyebrow. 'Does that sound too fanciful?'

'Not at all,' said Phoebe softly, her eyes fixed on the sleek animals tumbling around on the lawn. 'And this is magic. Thank you for sharing it with me.'

'It's worth sharing,' he said simply. 'A rare treat.'

It was rather unreal, Phoebe thought, standing beside this man who was a stranger, feeling in complete accord with him and curiously at ease. She wanted the moment to go on for ever.

But it was at that very moment that the vixen stopped playing with her young, raised her head, lifted her pointed, sensitive snout into the air and sniffed. Her nostrils quivered.

'She's heard something; can smell something,' Josh muttered. 'Somebody's coming.'

They held their breath and strained their ears but could hear nothing. Then, from a distance, came a faint hum and a milk float appeared down the drive, approaching the humpback bridge.

In an instant the fox family was gone, streaking away across the wide lawn before vanishing into a small copse of trees.

The garden was suddenly empty.

Josh turned abruptly from the window.

'Well, that's that,' he said flatly. 'The magic show's over. It's back to reality.'

He moved toward his desk as he spoke and indicated with a wave of his hand that Phoebe should take the chair opposite him.

His abruptness and instant dismissal of the delightful interlude astonished her. Could it all have been an illusion, the contentment, the feeling of security that had encompassed her as she had stood beside him? Why should he become all at once a different man to the one who had been bewitched by the foxes moments before? It was almost as if he felt guilty for being briefly relaxed and happy.

The smile had gone from his lips and his eyes, which had been full of warmth as he watched the antics of the wild creatures, were in an instant fathomless, deep blue pools as he stared at her across the desk.

The shutters had come down. It was a remarkable metamorphosis. Was it because he had suddenly remembered that she was a new employee and he regretted having revealed to her the gentler, vulnerable side of his character?

The thought saddened her and, in a dim sort of way, scared her a little. Once again she wondered what she was to expect from this perplexing man, with his swift changes of mood.

His thick eyebrows came together in a frown. He said curtly, 'The agency has faxed me through your references—our machine was on the blink yesterday—and I've had a chance to study them. I have to say that they're excellent and confirm what I'd already been told verbally. But, tell me, why, as a successful staff nurse— probably in line for a sister's post—have you opted out of a distinguished London hospital to take up agency nursing?'

The question totally surprised her. It was the last thing that she had expected. Why should he want to know that? 'D-does it matter to you?' she stammered. 'It has nothing to do with my ability as a nurse.' She pulled herself together and said firmly, 'As a matter of fact I just wanted a change; I felt I was getting stale. In the current climate of the health service a sister's post seemed a long way off.'

She was damned if she was going to tell him that she had fled from London because she had been hurt and disillusioned and had split up with her partner. That was her business and had nothing to do with him.

Josh raised his eyebrows. 'Really,' he said slowly as if he had read her mind. 'So you're not having an emotional crisis of any sort that might interfere with your work here?' His eyes bored into hers.

'I've no wish to pry but I do have a right to know if you have a problem—to protect my patients. They need emotionally stable people around them to give them support. Some of them are here for months on rehabilitation courses after having suffered severe trauma of mind and body. Of course it is no bad thing to have some life experience—it could be of benefit to the patients—but if you have personal problems I'd like to know about them now and not when it's too late.'

The nerve of the man. He can talk, thought

Phoebe; he's obviously got problems of his own, though he must successfully hide them from the patients. Well, he's not the only one who can put on a front. She raised her chin and stared back at him steadily and, keeping her voice low and even, said, '*If* I had any personal problems, Dr Richmond, I wouldn't let them come between me and my work. I'm a professional nurse and put my patients first always.'

'Good, I'm glad to hear it.' He leaned forward and put his elbows on the desk, made a steeple of his hands and studied her in silence. He noted the shining cap of mahogany hair, the high, slightly flushed cheek-bones, small retroussé nose, gold-flecked brown eyes and wide, generous mouth. A lovely mouth, he thought. And he liked the way her soft, warm eyes met his so directly and unwaveringly. Altogether it was a beautiful, gentle face, full of character. Gut feeling told him that she was right for Richmond Place, whatever her reasons for being there. After a few moments he said, 'Right, a month's trial and if you're suitable a longer contract.'

Phoebe stiffened. Another wave of anger suffused her. She clenched her hands until her knuckles were white. His arrogance was unbelievable. How dared he assume so much? She said coldly, 'The agency doesn't normally contract staff out for long periods and, anyway, I'm not sure if *you* will suit *me*.'

His mouth quirked at the corners and warmth flickered in his eyes. '*Touché*,' he said and added with emphasis, 'Then let me rephrase that remark—*if* we suit each other I'll come to some arrangement with the agency about a longer contract. Will you go along with that?'

She paused for a second and then nodded slowly. 'Yes,' she said. 'I can go along with that.'

She would like to have said that she'd think about it but admitted to herself that, in spite of his autocratic manner and fluctuating moods, she wanted to stay put at Richmond Place. It had so much to offer, both on a personal and a professional level. Here, in these idyllic surroundings, she was confident that she could come to terms with the anguish of the last year or so and fulfill herself as a nurse.

'Splendid.' He was relaxed and smiling as he stood up. 'Shall we shake on it and seal the bargain?'

Phoebe nodded again and found her hand

clasped firmly in his. He released it after a moment and said briskly, 'Now I want you to go and give Maeve a hand in the dispensary, dishing out meds and so on. It'll give you a chance to meet people. Then you can join me later for surgery. After surgery I'll be examining the new patients who were admitted yesterday.'

'How did your meeting go with the boss?' Maeve wanted to know when Phoebe joined her in the dispensary a few minutes later. 'Was he in one of his cool, distant moods?'

'Well, he was at times but he thawed after a bit; in fact, he was quite friendly.' But she said nothing about the fox interlude; it seemed too intimate, too personal, and she was sure that Josh expected her to keep it to herself—a private thing between them, even though he had ended it so abruptly.

'Well, I told you that his bark was worse than his bite and that, generally speaking, he's a *darlin'* man to work for,' her friend replied, emphasising her usually faint Irish accent.

The dispensary was busy and Josh had been right—she did meet many patients in addition to those she had met the day before in the activity centre. Nearly all the residents were on some sort of medication and most of them called at the dispensary to collect their pills and potions or receive injections before pursuing their plans for the day.

But several people were temporarily room-bound for one reason or another and by the time Phoebe had helped Maeve deliver their medicines it was time to join Josh in his surgery.

Josh's surgery, comprised of an ante-room, waiting-room and consulting-room, was next door to the dispensary in a large alcove just off the main corridor. Maeve, pointing it out when she had been showing Phoebe around, had said, 'Josh's holy of holies, where he listens and talks and generally offers comfort and advice; less a surgery than a sort of super-confessional.'

The 'confessional' was spacious, light and airy. It was well furnished, with a handsome dark oak desk, several squashy-looking arm-chairs, soft green velvet curtains at the tall windows and thick, mushroom-coloured wall-to-wall carpeting. There were shelves crammed with medical books on either side of the window and a bowl of fragrant pinks on the window-sill.

A screen of oyster-coloured pleated silk, to

one side of the room, partly concealed an examination couch, an instrument trolley and a wash-basin, the only evidence of a run-of-the-mill surgery.

Josh was sitting at the solid Victorian desk, writing, but he looked up as she entered. His eyes, very blue and unwavering, met hers across the width of the room.

'Do come in and sit down,' he invited, rising from his chair.

A nice gesture, Phoebe thought. Arrogant he might be at times but his manners couldn't be faulted.

He had changed since she'd seen him earlier when he had been wearing a track suit; now he was casually well dressed in a navy blazer worn over a snowy white open-necked shirt, revealing a cluster of bronze, curly hairs at his throat. With his thick tawny mane of hair and his neatly clipped, close-cut beard he looked rather nautical; not in the least daunting but large, calm and reassuring.

'How does it strike you?' he said, waving a hand round the room. 'It's just been refurbished.'

'As warm, welcoming, comfortable.'

He looked pleased. 'That's the general idea—to make people feel uninhibited so that they can talk freely and not be hassled; so much of our work lies in listening that it's often the best therapy. Outside surgery hours I make myself generally available to residents who just want to talk; they can make an appointment or just call in if I'm free. I try to keep it as casual as possible.

'Surgery itself is made up of the usual range of minor problems; sore throats, tummy upsets, earache and so on. People just turn up for advice and treatment. But I also do regular progress check-ups after surgery and these are booked in. One way and another the mornings are quite busy.'

'For you, certainly, but what do I do?' Phoebe asked.

'Assist in general. Help those who can't manage to get undressed if I need to examine them. Sort out record cards—they're kept in the locked filing cabinet in the ante-room. Book in follow-up appointments, arrange for blood and urine tests for you or Maeve to deal with at the end of the session or the following day. Bloods have to be done for despatch to the laboratory at Heresham Hospital by midday so should be booked in early. Believe me, you'll be busy enough most days.'

'Will I?' she asked doubtfully. 'It doesn't seem much after the hectic routine of a hospital ward.'

'But that's only the background—basic nursing stuff,' Josh said almost dismissively. 'Any competent nurse can do that.' He got up and moved round the desk and, leaning against it, looked down at her thoughtfully.

She returned his look, very conscious of his nearness and the scent of his cologne, sharp and astringent. He must have rubbed it into the silky stubble of his beard when he trimmed it, she decided, and then thought in a curiously detached fashion as she had once before: I wish he didn't have a beard; he's got such a strong face he doesn't need one. I'm sure he has nothing to hide.

There was a few moments' silence as they stared at each other and then Josh said in a firm voice, 'But you'll find your *real* work much more satisfying and fulfilling; you'll need all your skills as a person as well as a nurse. Learning to give old-fashioned, tender loving care to your patients without them feeling over-protected and patronised is quite an art; some of them are quite touchy about needing help.

'Most of them are eager and intelligent, striving for independence and equality despite their disabilities. Many are preparing to live on their own and it'll be your job to help them achieve that—give them the confidence to begin again.'

'It sounds an impossible task,' she said, fighting down a moment of panic. This wasn't the sort of nursing she was used to.

'It's not impossible but it's hard, exacting work and one tends to become emotionally involved, more than in hospital with short-term patients. That's inevitable, par for the job, but you have to learn when to switch off.'

'But I'm not trained in psychiatric nursing. Isn't that what they need? And surely they should have professional counselling?'

'That's always available but quite often people prefer to confide in someone they get to know and trust on a day-to-day basis. Not everyone finds psychiatric help acceptable and even with it they need other support.

'When I consider that you're ready I'll give you one or two patients to take a special interest in and you can work at forming a rapport with them. You'll find it a worthwhile two-way experience. They often have a lot to offer too; it's not all one-sided. It's friendship they seek and we *all* need friends, Phoebe, even those of us who are not obviously disabled, do we not?'

His eyes questioned her. He wanted her to agree with him. This was something that he clearly felt strongly about—his patient's emotional as well as physical needs.

What made him so perceptive and sensitive? she wondered, something that had happened to him in the past? Had he suffered both emotional and physical trauma? Is that why he identified with his patients so well; was so passionate on their behalf? And was he only talking about his patients? Was she imagining it or was he hoping for her understanding, her friendship, on a personal as well as a professional level? Is that what he meant by, 'we all need friends'?

Could this apparently self-sufficient man need her friendship? It didn't seem possible; they had only just met; they didn't know each other—and yet, in some peculiar way that she didn't understand, she felt drawn to him. Was that possible when he hadn't seemed even to like her at the scene of the accident? And she certainly hadn't liked him, with his icy blue eyes and arrogant manner. And even now she wasn't sure how she felt about him. He seemed patently sincere but was he just exercising his masculine charm to secure her loyalty to Richmond Place, to which he himself was devoted?

But, whatever his motives, he was right about the friendship bit; she couldn't argue with that. 'Yes,' she said softly, 'we all need friends.'

He nodded and said in a tone of quiet satisfaction, 'Good, I knew you'd understand.' Did he mean on a professional or personal level, or both? He pushed himself away from the edge of the desk and his hand brushed lightly against her bare forearm as he did so.

His accidental touch was like a tiny electric shock and took her completely by surprise. She gave a small, involuntary and, she hoped, imperceptible shiver and jerked her arm away. What on earth had made her react in such a fashion? The smile hovering round his firm mouth widened. Had he noticed her reaction? Was he mocking her?

No, of course he wasn't, she told herself

impatiently; she was imagining things. He was smiling because they were at one with each other; because they had achieved an understanding between them and he was genuinely pleased about it—nothing more.

He moved back round the desk and sat in his chair. 'Right,' he said briskly, 'by the sound of it we have customers waiting. Wheel in the first one, Phoebe, and let's play doctors and nurses.'

Surgery was exactly as Josh had described it— made up of minor ailments that were for the most part easily treated.

The first patient Phoebe recognised, as Maeve had introduced him to her the previous day. He was a retired, old-fashioned sort of army man in his eighties called Brigadier West. He had been severely injured when defusing a bomb some years after the war had ended. He was a tall, straight-backed, smart-looking man with a luxuriant, military-type, silvery moustache, twinkling hazel eyes, one arm and what he called his 'tin leg', though in fact it was a modern, well-made artificial limb which he managed admirably.

'The Brig,' Maeve had explained, 'is a

widower who comes every year for a few weeks' holiday in May and June. He manages so well on his own at home that he could go anywhere and stay in an ordinary hotel but for some reason prefers to come here. He's a great character, joins in many of the activities, chats with everyone, is a great morale booster and is a mean darts player.'

It was because he was such a darts fanatic that he had come to the surgery.

'I somehow managed to do something to my wrist when I was shaving this morning, God knows how. Twisted it or something,' he told Josh. 'It's damn painful, though I think it's only a sprain, but it's the only wrist I've got and I need it to beat those young chaps in a play-off tonight.'

After carefully examining the inflamed and slightly swollen wrist covered in paper-thin skin, Josh said with a reassuring smile, 'You're right, Brig, there doesn't seem to be anything broken; it appears to be only a sprain. You should rest it, of course, but if you're hell-bent on playing tonight we'll fit you up with something that should help you go forth and do battle.' He turned to Phoebe. 'I think a gentle massage with an analgesic cream, say Difflam, and a good firm bandage should do the trick, don't you?'

Phoebe nodded, pleased that he had asked her opinion. 'Yes, and a crêpe bandage covered by a Tubigrip wristband to give maximum support.'

'Good idea. You take Brig through to the dispensary and sort that out while I carry on here.'

On her return to the surgery Phoebe found Josh peering through an auriscope as he inspected the ears of a young woman in a wheelchair.

After a few moments he withdrew the auriscope and straightened up. 'Well, Ruth,' he said cheerfully to the pretty patient, who was looking at him with large, anxious eyes, 'you can stop worrying. I can assure you that you are not going deaf in the clinical sense. As far as I can see there's no anatomical or physiological defect; you're simply loaded with wax in both ears.'

'Oh, thank goodness for that,' said Ruth, letting out a huge sigh of relief. 'You see, both my parents went deaf at an early age and I thought I was going the same way.'

'Well, you're not, my dear; you can put that idea right out of your head. We'll put some drops in for a couple of days to soften up the wax and then one of my very efficient nurses,' he said with a grin, inclining his head in an ironical little bow towards Phoebe, 'will syringe your ears and you will be able to hear the proverbial pin drop.'

'That'll be brilliant. Thanks, Doctor,' said Ruth with a beaming smile, smartly pivoting her wheelchair to face the door.

'My pleasure. Go along with Nurse; she'll fix you up with drops and an appointment for the syringing.'

The next hour or so followed a similar pattern as Phoebe was kept busy making trips to and from the dispensary, renewing dressings to stubborn ulcers or slow-healing wounds, instilling eye drops and dispensing newly prescribed medication and making appointments.

As the morning wore on her appreciation for Josh, as a doctor, grew. He was sympathetic and understanding with every patient in a very matter-of-fact, down-to-earth way, with no hint of patronage. But he was surprisingly warm, too, and not afraid to show it when it was clearly what was needed. He was not at all impersonal. The cold remote man whom she had first met seemed to have vanished.

This was especially true when he examined the three new patients who had been admitted the day before, taking his time and putting them at their ease.

John Abbot, the young amputee who on his arrival had wielded his crutches so ably, was the last patient to be seen that morning.

Phoebe escorted him out of the consulting-room. When she returned to tidy up she found Josh, sitting at his desk and staring thoughtfully into space.

'I'm not happy about that young man,' he said, to her surprise.

'Really! But he seems so well adjusted; he seems to have come to terms with losing his leg. He's so cheerful.'

'Too cheerful,' said Josh drily. 'A keen footballer and wind-surfer. Unable to have a prosthesis fitted till his stump heals properly. Refused counselling. I reckon the poor lad's hiding something. What is he feeling guilty about? He had a motorcycle accident and his passenger was killed but apparently it wasn't even his fault. So why the guilt?' He looked at Phoebe questioningly.

'I've no idea,' she replied softly. 'I wish I had.'

'So do I, Phoebe,' he said feelingly, 'so do I.'

They parted soon after that—she to lunch with Maeve to sort out their afternoon duties and he, after thanking her for her help, to his paperwork in his private admin office.

'A never-ending chore,' he said with a wry smile as he walked slowly off down the long corridor, limping slightly.

As she got ready for bed that night Phoebe mulled over all that had happened during the day. It had started with the strange encounter with Josh in the morning when, in complete harmony, they had stood together watching the foxes and had ended with the unexpected meeting with his grandmother that evening in the lift.

She was a tall, elegant, elderly lady, straight-backed though she walked with two sticks. She had a mass of white hair piled on top of her head and eyes as blue as her grandson's.

'You must be our new nurse,' she'd said to Phoebe. 'Heard about you from Josh. I've been looking forward to meeting you, my dear. I'm Louisa Richmond.'

'And I'm Phoebe Palmer.'

Unable to shake hands on account of Lady Richmond's sticks, they had smiled and nodded to each other and when, moments later, they had reached the top floor she had invited Phoebe into her apartment for a drink. 'I always have a dry Martini at this time of day,' she'd explained cheerfully. 'And I do hate drinking alone so please take pity on an old lady and join me, that is unless you have other plans?'

Phoebe, pleased by the invitation, had murmured that, no, she was not doing anything until she went down to dinner and she would love to have a drink with Lady Richmond.

'Oh, splendid. Then come in and tell me all about yourself and your nursing and your plans for the future. I'm dying to know more about you. I like people and I'm a nosy old woman these days since I don't get out and about as much as I used to.' She had thumped her sticks on the floor impatiently and added, pulling a face, 'Arthritis, you know. Beastly condition; slows one up so.'

They had liked each other on sight and

Phoebe, generally used to keeping her own counsel, hadn't minded in the least answering the searching questions that she was asked. In fact, once she had started talking she'd realised how much she had needed to talk. She had kept her emotions bottled up inside herself for too long.

For Neil, even when their relationship had been at its most intimate, had never filled the role of confidant; the listening and the caring had all been on her side, although it had taken her a long time to realise it.

But, looking at the calm, kindly face of the elderly lady sitting opposite her, Phoebe had known instinctively that she'd cared; that she wasn't just being inquisitive. And, without quite knowing how it had come about, she'd found herself giving Lady Richmond a potted history of her life, though she'd said nothing of Neil— that episode was too raw, too recent. But she'd explained how her father had walked out when she was a small girl, leaving her mother to bring her up alone without help from anyone. 'My maternal grandparents were dead and my father's parents just didn't want to know,' she'd said sadly. Then, conscious that she might sound too pathetic, she'd hastened to emphasise what a very happy childhood she'd had.

'My mother was wonderful, so loving, though she never smothered me. I never felt deprived of anything. And as I got older she became my best friend as well as my mother. I was able to talk to her about absolutely everything. We had a brilliant relationship.'

' "Had"?' Lady Richmond had queried gently.

Phoebe had looked up from her drink and straight into the kind blue eyes fixed upon her. She'd taken a deep breath and said evenly. 'She died just over a year ago. Picked up an infection following a routine operation and died within days. It was devastating—the shock, you know. But I've come to terms with it now.'

'Have you? A year isn't long to accept that sort of loss, especially as you'd been so close, your best friend as well as your mother.'

'No, but I'm getting over it,' she'd said quietly, producing a tentative smile. 'And I'm sure that working here is going to help. The atmosphere is fantastic. I've so enjoyed my first day.'

'Well, my dear, I'm not surprised. A

satisfying job of work is the panacea to most ills,' Lady Richmond had replied and added, 'We all want to feel needed, useful, and we all need friends and that goes for our patients too. They don't always have to be on the receiving end, accepting help; however disabled they can offer friendship and that's being useful. Convince them of that and you will be halfway to helping them regain their dignity and self-esteem.'

They had been wise words, thought Phoebe, brushing her hair as she stood at the window staring out over the tranquil moonlit landscape. With her example to emulate, no wonder Josh is such a compassionate doctor. He and his grandmother make a super team, I only hope I can live up to them.

But though they had been last in her thoughts when she went to bed it was to dream, not of the Richmonds, but of Neil. A Neil with cold grey eyes, a cruel smile and unkempt black beard.

She woke in the morning with wet cheeks, a damp pillow and only a hazy memory of her dream.

CHAPTER FOUR

As the long, hot, sunny days of an almost tropical late May, punctuated by the occasional summer storm which kept the parkland and garden fresh and green, slipped quickly by and gave way to June, Phoebe settled into the routine. They were busy, satisfying days.

By immersing herself in work and other people's problems, she was able to blot out thoughts of Neil and suppress the dull, persistent ache in her heart. But, though it was relatively easy to do this during the day, the nights were more difficult. Alone in her room, memory haunted her and she could see his dark, bearded, handsome face vividly. And, recalling only what had been good in the early days of their relationship, she forgot his philandering ways and small deceits and their final bitter parting.

And occasionally, overwhelmed by loneliness and a regret for what might have been, she found herself weeping, not so much for her lost love but for her lost innocence and deep distrust of men.

But for the most part life became more manageable as the days passed.

Even the deep trauma and emptiness left by her mother's death she found more bearable, as one busy day succeeded another. Hard work was indeed proving to be something of a panacea to pain and heartache, just as Lady Richmond had suggested.

But it wasn't only the work itself, interesting and varying though it was, which helped her through each day but the special atmosphere that pervaded Richmond Place and touched everyone who lived and worked there. It was wrapped in an ambience of hope, to which even the most distressed patients began to respond after a time.

Staff morale was tremendously high; everyone from the cleaning ladies to the receptionists appeared to enjoy their work and joked and laughed as they went about their business. And as the days passed she realised that it was all down to Josh's influence.

In spite of her recently acquired cynicism about men in general, she recognised that he was a man who not only commanded respect but affection, too. She had been sure when she had first met him that he was cold, remote and full of resentment against the world and particularly against women.

But she knew now that this wasn't true. Certainly he had a natural reserve, an air of authority about him that prevented familiarity, but it didn't stop him being warm and friendly and there was no sign that he harboured a grudge against anyone, man or woman.

She began to see why he was so much admired by all who came in contact with him. He was rock-like, always there, endlessly on duty; a reassuring, strong presence, a caring doctor available to patients or staff at any time.

It was a revelation to Phoebe, coming from a vast, faceless, modern hospital where there was little or no contact with the people at the top and morale was shaky, to say the least.

There was no doubt that Richmond Place was special and she was lucky to be there and she threw herself into her work with enormous enthusiasm, finding herself looking forward to seeing Josh each day; for even if she wasn't working directly with him, knowing he was about and hearing his deep voice gave her confidence and a little jolt of pleasure.

And she was further uplifted by the renewal of her friendship with Maeve, who was always affectionate and cheerful and a joy to work with.

Together with the other trained staff, they shared the basic nursing duties, working alternate morning or evening shifts in the dispensary and assisting Josh in the surgery. But most afternoons, after doing dispensary and checking that all was well throughout the house, they worked independently in the gym or pool supervising and joining in various activities. Sometimes they made forays into the garden, talking to— or more often just listening to—residents who wanted to unburden themselves.

And how right Josh had been about that; listening *was* an all-important therapy.

'Probably better than any medicine that we can dish out,' Maeve said one day.

Phoebe agreed. It was great to have time to chat with patients; to be given the opportunity to do so and have it recognised as part of one's job and not a luxury extra.

But approving in general of this role of nurse counsellor didn't prevent her being shaken by the suggestion that Josh made one morning after they had finished surgery.

'Phoebe, leave that and sit down,' he said briskly, in what Maeve called his 'I must be obeyed', voice, as she pottered around tidying up after the last patient had departed. 'I want to talk to you.'

She sat down opposite him and meekly folded her hands in her lap.

Their eyes met across the desk. Phoebe returned the steady, direct look he was giving her just as steadily; she was now used to that clear, dark blue, sometimes enigmatic gaze, which she had earlier found unsettling.

She gave him a dimpling smile. 'Oh dear, you sound very stern,' she said. 'Have I done something dreadful? Is it a sin of commission or omission?'

He shook his handsome head and grinned broadly. 'Neither,' he said emphatically, 'quite the reverse in fact. You're doing so well that I've decided to give you a patient to take under your wing to make your special responsibility.'

Phoebe's eyes widened. 'Good Lord. Do you think I'm ready for that? I'm only just getting used to spending time listening and talking to people without feeling that I'm skiving.'

'And you're making a good job of it. It's really no more than good, old-fashioned tender loving care, you know, which so few places seem to have time for these days. I've watched you at work *and* I've been getting feedback from patients. You're already well liked, Phoebe, by both residents and staff. You fit in and you're a good listener, sympathetic but sensible and practical—not in the least bit sentimental—and the patients like that.'

Phoebe said tartly, 'Well, you've certainly been keeping tabs on me. I'd no idea.'

'I warned you at your interview that I would be watching you like a hawk and I make no apology for that. I had to make sure that you were right for us.'

'And as I seem to have passed the test you're willing to put a patient in my hands?'

He nodded and said with a rumbling chuckle, gently teasing, 'Indeed I am but, then, they're such neat, capable hands.'

Phoebe laughed too and, pleased with the small compliment, said a little breathlessly, 'Well, thank you, I'm glad you think so. So who is it that you want me to special?'

Josh looked down at a file on his desk. 'A Mrs Gillian Hallett; she was admitted when you were off duty.' He glanced up and asked, 'By the way, did you enjoy your days off? Go anywhere interesting?'

'Oh, yes, I had a great time exploring. I walked for miles on the downs. And went to Brighton and ambled round the Lanes and antique shops that I'd heard about. And, one evening, Maeve and I went to the Chichester Festival Theatre and saw a Noël Coward revival.'

'Do you like theatre?'

'Oh, yes, I do, very much,' she enthused. And then, quite suddenly and without warning, her treacherous mind flipped back to the shows she and Neil had seen together and the intimate suppers they had shared afterwards and she felt, for the moment, bereft.

She took a deep breath and snapped back into the present. 'We used to go frequently when I was at the Royal. It was easy, of course, being smack in the middle of the West End, surrounded by theatres, and as a bonus the hospital was sometimes presented with complimentary tickets so we didn't even have to pay the earth for seats.'

She hoped he would think that "we" meant medical and nursing staff in general and not herself and anyone in particular. No way did she want him to suspect that there had been any close involvement with anyone in her recent past that might conceivably interfere with her work. He had hinted at such at her interview and she had forcefully denied it.

Then she had been determined to get the job in the face of what she saw as his cool arrogance and chauvinistic dislike of women. *Now* she wanted to keep her job because she loved it and she wanted his respect and approval of her as a nurse.

Josh took her words at face value and accepted her explanation without question. 'Yes,' he said, 'we used to get freebies when I was an underpaid houseman at Central, an absolute boon as the cost of seats was so astronomical. Of course they're not quite as pricey down here and, though theatres are not thick on the ground, there are several decent ones within easy driving distance.

'And in the castle grounds at Monk's Chase

a few miles away they put on some superb out-door shows by visiting companies. They're doing *A Midsummer Night's Dream* in July and I'm taking some of the residents on a block booking. I'll need a few escorts and as Shakespeare isn't to everyone's taste I might be short-handed. Like to come and help out, Phoebe?'

His brilliant blue eyes caught and held hers. She stared into them and found herself unable to look away. Were they willing her to say yes?

Her mouth went dry and she couldn't speak for a moment. She felt breathless but exhilar-ated, her heartbeats drumming in her ears. Unseen threads seemed to be pulling her to him, closer, closer. She wanted to reach out and touch him, run her fingers through his mane of bright hair, but couldn't move. The room became hazy, very quiet and very still except for a slight breeze stirring the flowers on the window-sill and a bee buzzing round the blooms.

The moment seemed to go on and on, endlessly. . .

And then, a minute—five minutes—an unknown time later—his deep, rich voice filtered through from a long way off.

'Phoebe, you will come, won't you, and give me a hand?' he was saying as if nothing had happened.

And yet, surely, something *had* happened. Something had passed silently between them. But he looked and sounded his usual calm self; only his eyes seemed to her to betray some emotion for they had briefly darkened to indigo and had held an expression in them that she had never seen before and couldn't read. But the expression flickered and was gone in an instant and he sounded quite normal as he said, 'Well, will you come and help out or do you loathe the Bard?'

His words penetrated the cotton wool that seemed to be filling her head. What the *hell* had happened to her in those mind-blowing seconds and had it happened to him? Had she been hallucinating? Had it all been in her mind—that heart-stopping eye contact? Making a tremendous effort, she pulled herself together, found her voice and even managed a small smile. 'Yes, of course I'll give a hand; I'd love to. And, for the record, I'm quite a Shakespeare fan.'

'Ah, a fellow buff,' he said, beaming back at her. 'Great. I'm sure you'll enjoy the evening.

I'll let you know the details later.' He turned the pages of the file that he was holding in his hands. 'Right, now to business and Mrs Gillian Hallett.'

And Phoebe, damping down all intriguing personal thoughts, switched into professional mode and gave her full attention to what Josh was saying as he proceeded to give a precise account of the patient's medical history.

'Mrs Hallett is thirty-five and suffering from post-traumatic stress syndrome,' he explained in a carefully detached voice, 'a combination of emotional and physical shock following a radical mastectomy involving the complete removal of her right breast and associated lymph glands. To complicate matters her condition was further aggravated when her husband walked out on her.

'And that seems to have been far more devastating for her than her operation, poor woman. She's had a successful breast reconstruction but who the hell's going to help her reconstruct the rest of her life now that her bloody husband's deserted her?'

It was a rhetorical question to which there was no immediate answer.

After a pause he said, less angrily but with an edge of bitterness, 'She feels a freak; hates herself; blames herself for his defection. She blames herself for getting cancer—in fact, blames herself for everything that's gone wrong in their marriage, including the fact that they didn't have children. She's cut herself off from family and friends, almost as if she's afraid of contaminating them with what she sees as her inadequacies. She's reached an all-time low, Phoebe, and badly needs a confidante. Will you take her on?'

'Of course, if you think I'm capable. But I'm an amateur. Surely she needs to see a professional, a psychiatrist?'

'Seen one,' he said tersely. 'Didn't take to him; convinced it didn't help and has refused to see anyone else. But when I explained our ''befriending'' service she agreed to give it a try.'

'But why me, Josh? Why not yourself or Maeve or someone who's more experienced at it?'

He didn't answer at once but looked at her thoughtfully as if considering carefully what he was going to say. He rubbed at his beard with long, sensitive fingers. She wished he wouldn't do that: the gesture reminded her poignantly of Neil at his most calculating. With a mental shrug she dismissed the unpleasant memory and waited for Josh to answer her.

After a moment he said in a level voice, 'Well, my dear Phoebe, you're the ideal candidate. You've recently sustained a loss and are coming to terms with it and can identify with Gillian and appreciate what she is going through, having lost her self-respect and her husband. You're tuned in, as it were, and can empathise with her.'

Phoebe felt the blood leave her cheeks. Her heart bumped wildly. Her mind raced. Her loss! He must know about Neil but how? Nobody here knew about him; she'd not said a word— not even to Maeve. Perceptive as he was, he might have guessed at a broken relationship but he couldn't *know*, not for sure. And yet he spoke as though he knew what she had suffered—the indignity of rejection.

Had he been in touch with her old hospital and asked about her history or met someone from there who had told him the story of her break-up with Neil? A story that had whizzed round the hospital grapevine and had been much embroidered *en route*; a nine days' wonder which she had ended by resigning.

A wave of anger mixed with sadness washed over her. She hoped fervently that he hadn't gone ferreting out information about her. She'd thought that they had established an understanding, a trust, of each other.

But surely he did trust her or he wouldn't have asked her to special Mrs Hallett! Well, there was no point in prolonging the agony. If she wanted to know how he had come by his information she would have to ask. Not that there was anything he could accuse her of. She had perhaps misled him at her interview when she had denied any emotional entanglements. But she had promised then that nothing in her past would affect her work and it hadn't so he had no cause for complaint.

Not that he seemed to be holding anything against her—quite the reverse. For whatever version of the story he had heard he clearly didn't blame her for what had happened. His manner was gentle and compassionate and his blue eyes kind and understanding. But it wasn't enough that he seemed satisfied with what he had learned, she had to know how he had come by his information and whether by accident or design.

She looked at the composed, handsome face opposite her, quietly surveying her, and in a steady but rather strained voice asked, 'How did you find out what happened? I haven't talked to anyone about it.'

Josh said quietly, 'But you have. You told Grandmother and she put me in the picture. She thought I should know that you were still grieving for your mother, with whom you'd had such a special relationship. Why didn't you tell me at your interview, Phoebe? I would have understood. I knew there was something bothering you but I didn't know what.'

Phoebe stared at him in utter amazement and relief as she took in what he was saying. She was safe from further interrogation. He knew nothing of her affair with Neil—his concern had been all for her sadness, the loneliness, caused by her mother's death. That was the loss he was referring to. She didn't have to explain herself. He was satisfied with what he knew about her professionally and personally and felt that her experience would help her help one of his patients.

Ironically, for one wild moment, she felt like confiding in him and coming clean about Neil, sure that he would understand. The moment passed. One day she might tell him all but not yet.

She took a deep breath. 'I didn't want to talk about it, Josh. You were rather fierce, you know, when you interviewed me about not having any hang-ups that might interfere with my ability to do the job.'

'But you didn't mind telling Grandmother; she managed to wheedle it out of you!'

'Yes. It was easy to confide in her.'

He grinned. 'She's an old witch,' he said, his voice warm with affection. 'She has that effect on people.'

'You're very fond of her, aren't you?'

He smiled and his eyes gleamed. 'Think the world of her. She's a grand old lady. Took on me and my elder brother when our parents were killed in an earthquake when I was three and Laurie was five.'

'Oh, how dreadful to be orphaned when you were both so young.'

He shrugged. 'It wasn't the trauma that it might have been because frankly, we hardly knew our parents. We didn't have daily contact with them. They were passionate archaeologists always away on digs in remote parts of the world. Laurie has followed in their footsteps—he's in South America at the moment.'

'But archaeology didn't appeal to you?'

'No, not at all. I always wanted to do medicine like my grandfather. It came naturally to me. There've always been medical men in the family since way back. That's why Grandmother converted the manor into a rehabilitation home when Grandfather died—as a memorial to him and his predecessors.'

'Oh, what a lovely thing to do,' said Phoebe. 'And so practical.'

'Grandmother's a very practical lady,' replied Josh, his voice full of pride. 'But a romantic too. She and Grandfather met when she was nursing as a member of the VAD at the tail end of the First World War.' His mouth twisted cynically for a moment. 'You know, nineteen-fourteen to eighteen, the Great War that was to end all wars.

'She was just eighteen and apparently they

fell in love at first sight and remained in love till he died at the end of the thirties. Her single regret is that she only had one child, my father, and he wasn't interested in medicine.'

'It must please her immensely that you choose to work here as medical director instead of pursuing a career in a large hospital,' said Phoebe. She regretted the words as soon as she had spoken them, realising that they might be interpreted as implying that he was doing Lady Richmond a favour at his own expense.

Which is exactly how he did seem to interpret it for he frowned fiercely at her and said sharply, flatly, 'It pleases both of us.'

'Oh, Josh, of course it does. I can see that now. I didn't mean that you shouldn't. . .' Her voice trailed off and she looked at him help-lessly.

His eyes were suddenly cold. His lip curled in a cynical smile and he said drily, 'I think that's precisely what you *did* mean, Phoebe. You were saying to yourself—what the hell's a well-qualified doctor in his thirties doing bury-ing himself in a mundane rehabilitation unit in the middle of the country instead of fighting his way to the top in a high-powered teaching hospital—am I right?'

She nodded. 'Yes,' she said, in a low voice. 'Quite right. I did think that when I first came here and I still wonder what made you change direction. But there's nothing mundane about Richmond Place; it's very special and that's down to you. I can't imagine it without you at the head—you're needed here.'

'Thank you.' He paused. 'But. . .?'

'But when I first met you at the scene of the accident I assumed you were a surgeon. You acted like one, very much in charge—' she smiled slightly '—rather arrogant, even, but very reassuring too. And I admired the way you worked on that young woman driver; your hands were so good, so sure. And then I learned that you weren't a surgeon and it seemed such a waste.'

'And now. . .?'

'Now I know that the work you are doing here, helping to put together fractured emotions, is as vital and important as putting together fractured bodies and the two are often interdependent.' Her lovely, luminous brown eyes met his across the desk and her wide mouth curved into a gentle smile.

'And I also know,' she said softly, 'that your arrogance is only skin-deep and you'd probably make a rotten surgeon. You'd get too involved. You're interested in the whole person, not just the mechanical bits and pieces.'

There was a moment's silence and Phoebe wondered if she had gone too far, been too personal. His face was immobile, giving nothing away. Was he angry? Had she touched a soft spot? Did he sometimes hanker for the wider world of hospital medicine? Is that why sometimes his eyes looked bleak and sad when he was caught off guard? In spite of what he had said was he here on sufferance rather than by desire, a question of duty to his grandmother and the family name?

But her fears were groundless; she hadn't gone too far. Josh tilted back his head and chuckled quietly. 'So,' he said, 'you've sussed me out. I'm just a big softy, not tough enough to be one of the glamour boys of medicine—a top-notch surgeon.'

Phoebe shook her head and laughed. 'I take that back. I think you could be a top-notch anything that you wanted to be,' she said firmly. 'And you *can* be hard and tough when necessary. But surgery's not for you, Josh. You belong here, running Richmond Place. You're an inspiration to patients and staff—kind, calm and confident.'

She blushed a little as she finished speaking, wondering if she had sounded too fulsome—as if she was making up to the boss. No, she assured herself, she was just being honest, giving praise where praise was due and he would accept it as such.

He smiled and inclined his head. 'Well, thank you, I've. . .' The telephone shrilled loudly, insistently. He pulled a face and raised his eyebrows and the nostrils of his fine aristocratic nose flared. 'Damn,' he said, explosively. 'End of conversation, I'm afraid. I believe this is a call I've been expecting; it's going to take some time.'

'And I must go,' said Phoebe, standing up and moving away from the desk. 'I've masses to do.'

As she reached the door he said in his deep, velvet-soft voice, 'Phoebe, I'm glad we've had time to talk—it's been illuminating, to say the least. I feel we've learned a lot about each other.

You're a super nurse and you've got a lot to offer. Just go on being your usual kind, sensible self when you're dealing with Mrs Hallett.'

Phoebe nodded and let herself out of the room.

Though years of training enabled her to conceal her feelings, as she went about her work she was filled with a curious, bubbling elation after her long conversation with Josh.

But just below the surface calm her mind was busy, going over what they had said to each other—and not only said: her heart gave a little lurch as she remembered the eye contact episode. That had been extraordinary. It seemed almost unreal now, in retrospect, almost as if it had never happened. And yet it *had* occurred; there had been some curious meeting of their minds. They *had* been drawn together for a fleeting moment. Whether it had made the same impact on Josh she had no idea but it had certainly made an impression on her.

The afternoon was hot, sticky and oppressive. Too hot for anyone to want to walk or sit outside. A brassy blue sky arched over the empty parkland and garden. There was an occasional very distant rumble of thunder.

Maeve was off duty and Phoebe, after finishing the afternoon dispensing, set off to do the routine round of the house and check that all was well. It didn't take her long to tour the ground floor. She spoke to several people who were still resting but found, as she had expected, that some beds were empty. Their young, energetic occupants, disregarding the heat and their various disabilities, were already in the gym or the pool. She would catch up with them later.

She called at the reception desk when she had finished the ground floor round to establish who had booked out for the afternoon.

The flower-filled hall, smelling faintly of wax polish and roses and honeysuckle, looked as cool and inviting as it had on the day she had arrived three weeks before and Kathy Martin, who was on duty, looked just as cool and well groomed as she had then, in spite of the heat. 'There aren't many out today,' she said. 'Only ten—it's too hot for most of them to venture forth. Just as well; there's going to be one hell of a storm later.' She handed Phoebe a printed list of the people who had booked out. 'As you can see, they're all short-stay holiday people. No escorts needed.'

Phoebe stayed and chatted for a few minutes, enjoying Kathy's pithy, but never unkind, remarks about staff and residents, before making her way up to the first floor.

She would, she decided, finish her round of the first floor with a visit to Gillian Hallet and introduce herself and hopefully sow the seeds of friendship with her, as Josh had suggested.

She walked slowly down the wide, softly carpeted corridor which was, as always at this time of day, quiet but today, almost eerily quiet. Most of the doors were shut and these, as per Josh's instructions, she ignored.

'We must never forget,' he had explained when discussing the nursing routine with her when she had first arrived, 'that the people who come here come of their own volition and are entitled to privacy if they want it. We may think of them as patients but they are guests, too, and must be treated as such. Our role is to care for them with the minimum of intervention.'

It was a role to which she was slowly becoming accustomed but sometimes the conventional nurse in her longed to open a door to make sure that all was well. And she felt that urge today more strongly than usual. Perhaps it was the oppressive heat, which seemed to bear down on the building and even penetrate the dim relative coolness of the corridor, that made all her instincts bristle and warn her that something was wrong—made the hairs on the back of her neck stand up.

She stopped and listened outside each closed door. There was a murmur of voices behind one of the two-bedded rooms and a radio, playing soft music behind another but from most rooms there came not a sound.

Phoebe reminded herself, as she frequently did, that there were emergency bells in all the rooms that buzzed and flashed a light above the door and connected with Reception, Josh's office and the dispensary. Help could be summoned within seconds.

It was ironic that at that very moment as she was reassuring herself that all was well a light above a door near the end of the corridor began to flash. Her initial instinct had been right; something was wrong!

CHAPTER FIVE

As PHOEBE hurried toward the room she did an automatic assessment of the occupants in mental shorthand. Una Archer, fiftyish, post-hysterectomy convalescent. Could she be in difficulties—an internal haemorrhage perhaps? Not likely but possible. She quickened her step. The other patient was Fliss Brownlow, twenty eight, post viral infection syndrome, probably ME, normally fit, active, athletic; at present bone weary, lethargic and exhausted. Not a very likely subject to trigger off an emergency.

Phoebe reached the door in seconds and opened it wide, not knowing what she would find and well aware that it might *not* be a true emergency at all but something quite trivial.

That it wasn't trivial was obvious as she took in the tableau before her. Ashen-faced, Fliss, clad only in her bra and briefs, was sitting on the side of her bed clutching the top of her leg near the groin, from which thick, dark red blood was slowly oozing in a steady stream between her fingers down her thigh and onto the floor. Una was sitting bolt upright on her own bed, her face expressing shock and horror as she stared across at Fliss, her finger still on the emergency buzzer on her locker.

All this registered in the second it took for Phoebe to move from the door to Fliss's bed. Experience told her that she was looking at a ruptured blood vessel, not an artery—a vein because of the dark blood and because of the position near the groin: the long saphenous vein, she guessed.

Automatically she went into action. 'It's all right, Fliss,' she said calmly. 'Keep your hands there. Press hard with the palm of your hand. I'm going to roll you back onto the bed. I want you to lie flat.' With swift economical movements she lifted Fliss's legs, swivelled them round and eased her into the middle of the bed and then pulled the pillow from under her head. 'Lift up, love, if you can, so that I can put this under your bottom,' she explained, and added reassuringly, 'It'll help slow up the bleeding.'

She was only vaguely aware that someone else had come into the room and glanced up to see Josh standing at the other side of the bed.

'Here, let me,' he said, lifting Fliss up effortlessly so that Phoebe was able to slide the pillow in place beneath her thighs and buttocks.

She flashed him a smile of thanks and a flicker of relief surged through her at the reassuring sight of him and the sound of his voice. She knew that she could deal competently with the situation but two pairs of hands were better than one and it was great to have him there.

They worked together competently, anticipating each other's actions. Josh deftly took over applying direct pressure to the busted vein, releasing Fliss's shaking hands. Then, sitting down on the edge of the bed, he raised her foot and rested it on his shoulder.

Quickly Phoebe took a handful of tissues from a box on the locker, folded them into a thick square and handed it to him to use as a pressure pad. Then, using the remainder of the tissues, she cleaned the worst of the blood from Fliss's hands, whilst murmuring reassuringly to her and Una. For Una, who had at last taken her finger from the buzzer and was lying back against her pillows watching them with anxious eyes, was almost as distressed as Fliss.

'I'm going to need another pressure pad,' Josh said in a low voice. 'Something more substantial.'

'A towel,' said Phoebe and, opening the door of the bedside locker, fished one out which she folded into a neat, thick pad and handed to him in exchange for the sticky wad of blood-soaked tissues, which she dropped into the wastepaper bin.

The thick pad enabled Josh to apply better direct pressure to the ruptured vein and after a minute or so the bleeding slowed considerably but, in spite of this improvement, Fliss was beginning to show signs of shock. She was pale and clammy and shivery. Phoebe fetched blankets from the linen cupboard and tucked one round her chest and shoulders. 'Thanks,' mumbled Fliss, managing a faint smile, 'that's great.'

Josh said softly, 'Hang on in there, my dear. You're doing fine. The bleeding's definitely easing up. You'll soon begin to feel more comfortable now that you're lying flat and are warming up and getting some blood circulating properly. But I must tell you, Fliss, that this is only first-aid stuff and, as soon as we can, we've got to get you off to hospital.'

'Do you mean that you can't treat me here?' Her eyes were large and anxious.

'Sorry, afraid not, love.' His voice was firm but gentle.

'You need intravenous fluids and surgery to repair the vein. And you'll probably have investigations to find out what caused this spontaneous rupture. It doesn't appear to be connected with your general condition and there's been nothing in your recent blood tests to indicate what might be wrong. But the hospital may come up with some clues—there are some brilliant physicians and surgeons there. You'll be in good hands.'

It was at this moment that two care assistants, Mary Mead and Ken Summers—having been contacted by Kathy from Reception—put in an appearance.

Josh immediately sent Mary to fetch the emergency bag from the dispensary and Ken to phone for an ambulance. 'Put them in the picture, Ken. Quote me and emphasise that this is an emergency—a serious venous haemorrhage with the patient conscious but in shock,' he said in a low voice. 'That should bring them stat. . .

Tell them that I'll speak to the casualty officer at Heresham as soon as possible and fill him in on the details.'

'Will do,' said Ken as he left the room.

Mary returned with the emergency bag and a mobile oxygen cylinder and mask.

Josh nodded his thanks. 'Good,' he said. 'Now, Phoebe and I will carry on here. You take Una downstairs and give her a cup of something hot and sweet; she deserves it.' He looked across at Una. 'Thanks for your help, Una, buzzing for us so promptly. You helped save the day.'

Una blushed. 'Is Fliss going to be all right?' she asked.

'She'll be fine but she needs specialist treatment and will have to go into hospital for a few days.' He smiled down at Fliss. Then, keeping the pressure pad in place with one hand, he ran the other down the injured leg, pausing to feel behind the knee for the popliteal pulse to test the volume of blood passing through the artery. 'That's not too bad,' he said. 'How are you feeling now, Fliss?'

'Better but I'm still cold.'

'We can soon remedy that. Phoebe, another blanket.'

Phoebe, having anticipated him, had a blanket at the ready which she tucked round Fliss's good leg and foot. For a fraction of a second Josh looked straight into her eyes and for a fleeting moment she fancied that there was something of the magic of their eye contact that morning.

Una's voice broke into the moment. 'Does she *have* to go into hospital? Can't you look after her here?' she asked, sounding quite aggressive.

'No, we can't do surgery here; we haven't got a theatre,' Josh explained patiently, recognising her nervous tension. 'But we will be able to look after her as soon as she's had hospital treatment and she should be back with us quite soon.'

'Oh, I do hope so.' Una slid off her bed, slipped on a pair of sandals and padded over to kiss Fliss on her pale cheek. 'Good luck, love. See you soon,' she said and, rather reluctantly, allowed Mary to steer her out of the room.

'Right,' said Josh to Fliss as soon as they had departed. 'The first thing we're going to do is to give you a whiff of oxygen, which will make you feel less faint and help you to breathe better. Let's have it please, Phoebe.'

Phoebe switched on the small cylinder of oxygen and placed the mask over Fliss's face. 'Now slow, deep breaths,' she instructed and nodded with satisfaction as Fliss complied.

Josh nodded too. 'Good,' he said. 'Now let's replace this makeshift pad with a proper haemostatic dressing. That's a prepared pad to help control the bleeding,' he explained to Fliss. 'Look out a Keltostat dressing, Phoebe. We'll try that and secure it with a pressure bandage.'

They were fixing the dressing in place when Ken returned.

'The ambulance will be here shortly,' he said. 'There's one available on the Heresham Road.'

A little over half an hour later the ambulance, with Fliss on board accompanied by Mary Mead, moved away down the drive and the storm that had been threatening all afternoon burst overhead, with a gigantic clap of thunder and a vivid flash of lightning.

Josh and Phoebe stood side by side under the portico, watching as the ambulance drove away.

'Get a taxi back after you've seen Fliss safely

settled in,' Josh had instructed Mary, handing her some notes as she was climbing into the ambulance.

'Is Fliss going to be all right?' Phoebe asked, staring after the departing vehicle.

'She'll do,' replied Josh, meaning that she wasn't at death's door.

There was another great crash of thunder, followed almost immediately by a zig-zag of white lightning as the ambulance crossed the humpback bridge. Within seconds a mixture of large globules of rain and hail began to beat down and bounce on the smooth golden gravel of the drive.

The empty park, stark and desolate, was shrouded in a purple-grey veil as the torrential rain poured down from an almost black sky. Under the portico it was as if dusk had fallen. The temperature dropped dramatically. Everything seemed unreal.

Phoebe thought, We are alone in the world, Josh and I. She wanted to touch him. She wanted him to touch her. It was the second time that day that she had wanted to be close to him. She shivered—there were goose pimples on her bare arms.

Josh said softly, turning towards her, his face dim in the half-darkness, 'Are you cold, Phoebe? Are you afraid of the lightning? Do you want to go in?'

She shook her head. 'No, not yet. I'm not really cold and I don't mind the storm. In fact it's a relief after the stifling heat this afternoon.'

He gave a deep throaty chuckle. 'It has a touch of the *déjà vu* about it, don't you think? You and storms and accidents seem to go together. After all, we met in a storm just three short weeks ago.' His hands were on her shoulders, turning her towards him. He bent his head. His strong, handsome, cologne-scented face was close to hers. His eyes glinted between half-closed lids in the dim light.

She felt light-headed, almost faint. She was overwhelmed by a desire to stroke the tawny, silky softness of the hated beard.

This is madness, she thought, her mind racing as she lifted her hand without meaning to and then let it fall. I've had enough of men and I don't like beards so what's the matter with me? I admire Josh as a doctor but as a man who attracts females as bees to a honey pot—just like Neil?

No, not like Neil. Neil was a womaniser but Josh rejects women on a personal level, doesn't he? Maeve had said that he'd never been known to have a date with anyone. Women haven't interested him since his unhappy affair and its mysterious, abrupt ending.

So why is he looking at me in such a strange, intense fashion? Is he about to kiss me? Do I want him to? She shivered again and took a step backwards. Josh's hands slid down her arms and imprisoned her wrists. 'Phoebe,' he said in his rich, velvet-soft voice, 'what's wrong? You're not frightened of me, are you?'

'No, no, of course not. It's just that. . .' Another ear-splitting crash of thunder rocked the ground and brilliant arrows of white-gold lightning streaked to earth from miles above them, seeming to be aiming straight for them and lighting up the park, lighting up the sky. In spite of not minding storms, she jumped as the thunder slammed and vibrated against the pillars of the portico and when Josh drew her gently towards him and wrapped his arms round her she neither tried nor wanted to resist.

He cradled her head against his vast chest and murmured reassuringly into her hair and she could feel and hear the steady thud of his heart beneath her ear. It was the first time that any man had held her in such a fashion—protectively not demandingly. It was a new experience. It was a wonderful feeling, a safe feeling. There had never been a man in her life who had held her so close. No father, grandfather, uncle or brother to provide strong, masculine, undemanding support.

Neil had certainly never provided that; he had been too sex-orientated, too selfish. If he had kissed her or put his arms about her it had been with bed in mind; he had had no time or inclination to comfort her. And, toward the end of their relationship, he hadn't even bothered to exhibit his famous charm that was a byword in the hospital and had held her prisoner for months.

In those last weeks only sex had held them together. He was good at that and had remained good at that till the end. And she had clung to it as to a lifeline, rather than lose him. In the early days she had enjoyed the sex, giving a lot and expecting little, content to be the object of his attention and of, so she had thought, his love. Love! She knew now that what she had experienced with Neil hadn't been love at all, even on her side, though she had thought it was at the time. It had been purely physical attraction that she had mistaken for love—a longing to love and be loved.

Not surprisingly she had succumbed to his advances readily. And they had seemed well matched. He with his lean physique, black beard and dark good looks and she with her bronzed chestnut hair, gold-flecked brown eyes and slim but softly rounded figure.

All these shadowy thoughts and memories whirled and swirled round in her mind as she stood in the circle of Josh's arms beneath the portico, while the storm raged round them.

How long they remained like that she had no idea but quite suddenly, as abruptly as it had arrived, the storm began moving away. The thunder still crashed and the lightning streaked earthwards but it was no longer directly overhead.

Reluctantly Phoebe stirred in Josh's arms: she had no excuse for staying there now. She lifted her head from the broad expanse of his chest and stared up at him. 'Thank you,' she whispered.

'For what?' he asked softly, smiling down at

her, keeping his arms wrapped tightly round her and holding her close.

Phoebe felt foolish, hardly knowing how to answer. She couldn't possibly reveal all her thoughts. She stammered, 'Well, for. . .for. . . making me feel safe.'

'Safe?'

'Yes.'

'From the storm?'

She nodded.

'But you're not afraid of storms.'

'No, I'm not generally but this was a particularly bad one. It seemed much worse than storms in town; everything looks so. . .so. . .desolate. Like the end of the world,' she finished uncertainly. 'And I felt so lonely, that is until you touched me, and you were—are—being so kind and understanding. . .' To her fury she felt tears well up and lowered her head to hide them from him.

Josh, keeping one arm firmly round her, raised his other hand and lifted her chin, forcing her to look at him. 'Don't be ashamed to cry, love,' he said in an incredibly tender voice. 'Tears are natural, a safety valve. Let yourself go for once; don't be so stoical. Give way; it helps sometimes. Talk if you want to.' His eyes searched her face. 'You're not just grieving for your mother, are you? There's something else. Tell me!'

'I can't,' she whispered. 'Some time perhaps but not yet.'

'All right,' he said quietly, his eyes looking steadily into hers. He loosed his arm from about her waist and she stepped back. 'Any time when you're ready, Phoebe, any time.' He leaned forward and brushed her forehead with his lips. 'Now, ready for work?'

She nodded.

'Right, then, it's once more into the breach,' he murmured, just as she had done when she had first arrived at Richmond Place a few short weeks before. Pushing open the massive front door, he steered her through into Reception.

I'm getting expert at smothering my feelings, thought Phoebe as, putting the memory of that fleeting kiss and the intimate moments she had just shared with Josh firmly behind her, she went about her evening chores with her usual cheerful efficiency.

With Maeve off duty she had the evening

dispensing to do and this took longer than usual as rumours of the afternoon's emergency were flying around and many people wanted to know about Fliss. She spent time reassuring them and satisfying their genuine curiosity. But eventually the session came to an end and she decided to visit Gillian Hallett as she had meant to do that afternoon. It was time to put her 'befriending' of that sad lady into action.

The first-floor corridor was busy with carers hurrying to and fro carrying trays from a pair of parked trolleys to those residents who had elected to eat in their rooms rather than go down to the dining-room. There was a hot and a cold trolley as good food properly served at the right temperature was a rule of the house.

'Has Mrs Hallett's tray gone in?' Phoebe asked Gwen Dunne, the senior carer who was presiding over the trolleys.

Gwen consulted a plastic-covered list. 'No, not yet. Why, have you got a treatment to do? Do you want me to hold it back?'

'No, I'm only going in for a chat. I'll take it with me, if I may. What's she having?'

'Chicken salad and a roll and lemon mousse—the same as she ordered last night—

and most of that came back untouched, as I remember,' replied Gwen, pulling a face.

'But perhaps that was because it was her first night here. I was going to check on her tonight to see if the same thing happened and let you or Maeve know if she still wasn't eating. She isn't down for a special diet but she's dreadfully thin; looks as if she could do with feeding up, as my old mum would say. Perhaps you can persuade her to eat tonight.'

'I'll do my best,' promised Phoebe, taking the tray but privately thinking that she was unlikely to be successful, knowing the depressed state that this particular patient was in.

From what she knew about Gillian Hallett she had lost interest in everything and this almost certainly included food. But she couldn't be seriously undernourished or Josh would have commented on it when he briefed her. He must have decided that if Gillian's emotional state could be improved she would automatically start eating better.

But that he considered food vitally important to a patient's well-being Phoebe was well aware for he had given her a lecture on the subject soon after her arrival at Richmond Place.

'Good food, fresh fruit and vegetables and a little of what the patient fancies is all part and parcel of treating the whole person,' he'd stated emphatically. 'We don't farm out the catering here: we prepare all our own food in our own kitchens and take pride in the cooking and its presentation. It's got to look good as well as taste good.

'And our staff are taught to note if patients eat well, not just plonk the food in front of someone and hope for the best. This is especially important where residents opt to eat alone. The odd occasion isn't important but if it becomes a habit then how well or badly they eat may reveal a great deal about their emotional and physical condition.'

She had been impressed by his enthusiasm for the subject. His extraordinary blue eyes had blazed at her across the desk. Then, quite suddenly, he'd grinned at her and pulled a face and said with a chuckle, 'Sorry about the lecture. Got carried away—rather a hobby-horse of mine, caring for the whole person and not just the bit of them that's obviously injured.'

Phoebe had chuckled too. 'I did wonder,' she

said. 'But it's a very practical hobby-horse. You're so right about food being important. It's a great morale-booster. And most of the big hospitals haven't got the time or the money to care about it these days. It's very low on their list of priorities, except, of course, for special diets.'

'Too true,' he'd said.

With that conversation fresh in her memory she made her way to Gillian's room. What a caring doctor Josh is, she thought. What a privilege it is to work for him. Nothing is too much trouble where his patients are concerned.

Or his staff, she reminded herself, slowing her step. A little glow of shy pride and pleasure stole over her and flushed her cheeks as she recalled how he had held her in his arms beneath the portico when the storm had raged and she had felt so alone and so vulnerable.

She had felt as safe as a child. He had been large, protective and comforting and yet so very masculine. His body had been hard and muscular and the smell of his cologne-scented beard had drifted down to her as she'd leant against his broad chest. Her nostrils flared. She could smell it now—tangy, exciting, sexy. . .

She had to knock twice at the door of room twenty-four before a low voice invited her to come in.

Gillian Hallett was sitting at a table by the window, staring out over the park glittering after the storm in the brilliant, slanting, evening sunshine. The lawns and shrubs quivered with a thousand prisms of light.

She didn't look round as Phoebe crossed the room but turned and glanced up at her as she set the tray on the table. 'Thank you,' she said tonelessly, her pale blue eyes, devoid of all expression, meeting Phoebe's briefly.

Tired, dead eyes, thought Phoebe, shocked by what she saw, or rather didn't see, reflected there. And there were pale blue-grey smudges beneath her eyes and her pale, lank blonde hair hung down about her face, which was gaunt and bony. It was a face that had once been classically beautiful—oval, with a high forehead, high cheek-bones and neatly moulded chin—but now looked like an empty, colourless mask.

Phoebe wanted to touch her, hug her, make her feel something and bring her to life but instinct told her that this wouldn't be welcome so instead she introduced herself. 'I'm Phoebe

Palmer,' she said quietly, holding out her hand. 'Dr Richmond asked me to visit you.'

'Oh.' The expressionless eyes met Phoebe's again and a frown creased the marble-white forehead. 'I don't understand.'

'The befriending service,' said Phoebe gently. 'You agreed to talk to me.'

'Oh.' She bent her head over the table and stared down at the tray of food. Her hair hung forward like a stringy curtain. 'I'd forgotten but I remember now.' She picked up her knife and fork and prodded aimlessly at a piece of chicken. 'He was very kind, Dr Richmond. He didn't badger me; didn't probe.'

'He wouldn't. He's a marvellous doctor and very perceptive.'

'He said you wouldn't probe either; that you would just listen *if* I wanted to talk.' Her fingers tightened round the knife and fork. 'You won't *make* me talk, will you?' she asked in a small voice. 'You won't psychoanalyse me, will you?'

Phoebe said gently, 'I wouldn't know how. I'm a nurse not a psychoanalyst. But I know from personal experience that talking can help but if you don't want to talk that's fine by me. I'd just like you to know that I'm around if you need me. Would you like me to pop in each day just to say hello? It'll be up to you whether we talk or not.'

Gillian pushed a piece of crisp, crinkly lettuce round her plate, then lifted her head and stared at Phoebe. The pale lacklustre eyes held a hint of interest. 'What do you mean, "from personal experience"?'

Phoebe hesitated. How much should she divulge about herself? Did she want to reveal anything personal to a patient? She had been taught to keep her personal problems to herself; to listen and observe but not to become too involved with those in her care.

But Josh had suggested that she try to help Gillian precisely because she had problems and was still coming to terms with the death of her mother. He'd thought it might help her to understand how alone and depressed Gillian was feeling after being deserted by her husband on top of her major operation.

And he was right, of course; it did. And though he didn't know it but had guessed at it she, like Gillian, had suffered a second loss when her relationship with Neil had ended. That made her all the more capable of understanding how rejected and inadequate the poor young woman felt.

So she shouldn't feel reluctant to disclose something about herself; let Gillian know that she, Phoebe, was vulnerable, too, if it was going to help her. She couldn't tell her about Neil but she could tell her about her mother.

She said softly, 'My mother died last year and she and I had been very close. There were just the two of us—no other relatives. I was shattered by her death. I felt guilty as if I had somehow let her down. I should have confided in a friend but for some reason I couldn't bring myself to talk to anyone about it. I tried to cover up my feelings and pretend that I'd come to terms with what had happened but. . .'

'But. . .?' Gillian still seemed interested; she was looking at Phoebe expectantly. Just to have got this much attention from her was something of a breakthrough.

'I didn't really come to terms with it until a few weeks ago when I met someone to whom I found I could talk.'

'A super-wise psychiatrist type, I suppose,' Gillian grated scornfully.

'No, a super-wise old lady,' replied Phoebe

evenly. It flashed through her mind that it was a pity that Lady Richmond was away on holiday. She would have been an ideal person to provide friendly counselling.

'You're saying that talking helped?'

'Yes.'

'But you weren't rejected. Your mother didn't *want* to die and leave you. You were just grieving for someone you loved. That's natural. You don't know what it's like to be really rejected by someone you love.

If only you knew, thought Phoebe.

'It wasn't your fault that your mother died but it was *my* fault that my husband. . .' Her voice died away to nothing and there was a moment's silence before she added in a whisper, 'I feel so worthless, so tired, and I look so dreadful, mutilated.' She touched the right side of her chest where her reconstructed breast swelled gently and realistically beneath the silk bodice of her dress.

'And look at my hair.' She ran a trembling hand through her lank tresses. 'No wonder my husband left me. What am I going to do? Can you help me?' She looked up at Phoebe, her eyes brimming with unshed tears.

'Well, I will if I can and if you'll let me,' said Phoebe in a calm, neutral voice, instinct again warning her not to overdo the sympathy. 'I can at least lend an ear. But if you'd rather talk to someone else, someone more experienced, Dr Richmond will arrange it.'

Gillian shook her head. 'No, I don't want anyone else,' she said wearily. 'You seem kind. . .and, well, caring, sensible, not pushy.'

'Thank you.' Then, hoping that she was saying the right thing, Phoebe said, 'But the sensible caring nurse in me *is* going to push a little and suggest that you try to eat something. It won't help if you starve. You're physically in poor shape and that must be adding to your depression, your tiredness, and it's certainly not helping your looks. Though all your hair needs to improve it is a good shampoo and conditioner. I can do that for you if you don't want to see the hairdresser.'

'Thank you.' Her voice was flat, expressionless, and her eyes were suddenly wary, defensive. 'But that won't be necessary. I can manage.'

Oh, hell, thought Phoebe, I've blown it. She's feeling pressurised. Phoebe had been told that people who were depressed often resisted help—it was part of their depression.

She shrugged and said ruefully, 'Sorry, I'm doing exactly what I promised not to do— pressing too hard. But I did tell you that I was no good at this psychology business. I was just trying to be friendly, helpful, practical.'

'It's all right. It doesn't matter. I know you mean well; everyone does.'

It was dreadful to hear the despair in her voice and see it in her eyes.

'Oh, my God, the last thing I want to be is a do-gooder and end up by doing more harm than good. I think you'd be better off with some-one else, Gillian. I'll have a word with Dr Richmond.' She backed away from the table. 'So sorry I couldn't be more help.'

There was a short silence as she walked across the room and then, just as she reached the door, Gillian cried out in a high, frightened voice, 'No, please don't abandon me. Come back tomorrow and let's talk again. I'm sorry I was so rude. Please say you'll come back, please...'

Phoebe stopped with her hand on the door-handle, took a deep breath and looked round over her shoulder. 'All right,' she said evenly, 'we'll give it another try. I'll see you tomorrow afternoon if that's what you want. Goodnight, Gillian.' She opened the door and, with a sigh of relief, stepped out into the corridor.

Head bent and deep in thought, she made her way slowly downstairs feeling absolutely drained of all emotion. She had been warned that befriending a traumatised patient was hard work—a refinement of tender loving care that was an exhausting process—but she hadn't appreciated how exhausting. It was like walking on eggshells, trying not to say or do the wrong thing.

'Sure, it's nothing like as simple as giving an injection or taking blood or slapping on a dressing,' Maeve had said at her most Irish. 'It's groping in the dark, listening, being endlessly patient, knowing you can't solve the problem, shouldn't even try. You can just be there and let the poor benighted souls find their own solutions. And the hell of it is that Josh's befriending service often works. He's a good and grand doctor.'

Phoebe lifted her head as she approached the foot of the staircase and, pausing on the next to bottom step, found herself staring straight into the brilliant blue eyes of Maeve's 'good and grand doctor'. Like a genie from a lamp, she thought wildly, and couldn't stop herself from giggling uncontrollably. 'I'm sorry,' she gasped. 'I don't mean to be rude. . .I was thinking about you and there you were.'

Josh chuckled. 'Like a genie from a lamp,' he said, seeming uncannily to read her mind.

Rooted to the spot, Phoebe drew in her breath sharply. 'You knew what I was thinking,' she said, accusingly. 'How did you know?'

'Sixth sense,' he hazarded. 'It's called shadow sight in the Highlands. I'm a Celt, you know, several times over. I've Scots, Welsh and Irish blood in my ancestry, not to mention a touch of the Cornish.' He held out a hand in a courteous, old-fashioned gesture, silently offering to help her down the last two stairs, and hesitantly she found herself sliding her hand into his.

And she was glad of his support. Her legs felt shaky as she descended. His hand felt large, warm and comforting and something more than that—an electric impulse seemed to flow through his fingers into hers. A curious tingling sensation ran up her arm and into her throat. She swallowed. Her heart thumped hard, fast and painfully as her breathing quickened and her breasts rose and fell rapidly, straining against the thin cotton of her uniform dress. Because he was touching her?

For a moment they stood silently facing each other at the foot of the stairs. The ancient reception hall was dim and quiet as a church as the westering sun slanted through the high windows, illuminating the dust motes.

Her head was tilted back as she looked up into his face. He looked magnificent. She was reminded again of the picture-book Viking. His blue eyes, so often unreadable, seemed to glitter hungrily down at her; his nostrils flared; his mane of tawny blond hair was an aureole round his large, handsome head and his lips gleamed moistly red above his bearded chin.

Surely this time he *would* kiss her, properly, on the mouth and suddenly she knew that she longed for him to do just that. But did he want her or was she deluding herself?

There was a dull ache in the region of her heart and for the second time that day she wanted to reach up and stroke his silky beard and for the second time she rejected the impulse. And it was then, at that very moment as she resisted the longing to run her fingers through the rich, tawny hair and feel the strong jaw beneath, that she knew that she was in love with him. Deeply and irrevocably in love.

CHAPTER SIX

IN LOVE! The thought stunned Phoebe. Impossible! The idea took her breath away. Speechless, she continued to stare up into Josh's face as her mind grappled with the ridiculous notion. She couldn't be in love. She had turned her back on love when she parted from Neil. It was just the need for reassurance that was attracting her to this bearded giant—her boss, who was kind and comforting but who could also be arrogant and aloof. She had to remember that. . .he was off women as much as she was off men.

He musn't guess at the jumbled thoughts that were racing through her mind. He must never know that she was in love with him. He would clam up and become even more remote and austere than he had been when she had first met him; and that she couldn't bear.

She forced herself to meet his eyes and, hoping that her own were unreadable, assumed a bland look and said breathlessly, managing a little laugh, 'I hope your shadow sight doesn't allow you to read *all* my thoughts.'

'No, alas, it doesn't. In any case that would be cheating but I don't need shadow sight to see that you look fraught right now. What's wrong, Phoebe? Can I help?' He was smiling down at her with the calm, compassionate look she had seen on his face when he was with patients. His eyes no longer glittered as they had seemed to do moments before. Now they were soft and gentle.

Could he help?

You could stop being so bloody *nice*, she thought savagely, and let yourself be ruthless and sexy and aggressive for once. The intensity of this desire to have him drop his comforting image and practically force himself upon her was mind-boggling. Surely the last thing she wanted was an aggressive, demanding man, even if she loved him! No, of course she didn't want aggression in any shape or form. Angrily she pushed away the alien thought.

What she did want was someone who was strong and fair-minded enough to treat her as an equal; someone who wouldn't patronise her and wouldn't cheat but who would be assertive or supportive as necessary.

Was Josh that man? Did any such man exist?

She strove to be calm but frustration and anger with herself for letting herself fall in love with him boiled up inside her. He must never suspect that she was uptight because of him. She must divert his attention; put him off the scent. Well, he wasn't entirely responsible for her looking fraught. There had been her session with Gillian, which had been distressing and exhausting.

She recalled those dead eyes, shivered and, laying the blame firmly at his door, blurted out accusingly, 'You shouldn't have asked me to befriend Gillian Hallett. I'm not experienced enough. I've just visited her and I feel awful, useless. I might have done her more harm than good. She's so desperately depressed, so unhappy.'

'Did she tell you so?' Josh asked.

Phoebe nodded.

'Then I'm sure you haven't done any harm,' he said firmly. 'Believe me, she wouldn't have confided that much if she hadn't wanted to. She would have remained silent. So stop castigating yourself.' He frowned.

'But I'm sorry you've been so upset by the

experience. Perhaps it was too much to ask of you to befriend such a difficult patient. But you're a splendid nurse—kind, sensitive, practical and good at the old tender loving care bit. And the fact that you've recently lost someone close to you seemed to make you an obvious candidate for the job.' He looked thoughtful.

'Error of judgement, I'm afraid. I was sure you could handle it. Perhaps I'd better take over Gillian's case myself. It's a pity but the last thing I want is for you to be further distressed when you are still grieving for your mother.'

All sorts of emotions washed over her. A thrill of happiness that he seemed to care about her. Fury that she had confessed to finding it difficult to handle a patient. But most of all the feeling that Gillian Hallett needed her and would feel rejected if she gave up on her—that she would be letting her down as well as Josh if she opted out now.

She pleaded urgently, 'No, don't do that. Give me another chance. I want to go on trying. I believe I may have begun to form a rapport with her—she wants me to visit again tomorrow.'

'Does she now? Well, that's progress. You

shouldn't be worried; you've done well.' He sounded pleased and satisfied and, taking her completely by surprise, cupped her chin in his hands and tilted her face up to his. 'And are you sure you can cope?'

'Yes.' She was very conscious of his firm but gentle hands on her skin which felt cool and clammy beneath his warm touch. I'm in mild shock, discovering that I'm in love with him, she thought. . . Emotional trauma—how odd.

He massaged her pale cheeks with his thumbs until she felt them beginning to tingle. His clear gaze searched her face. What was he thinking? Dear God, she prayed silently and fervently, please don't let me give myself away; don't let him see that I love him. And don't let him give me a kindly, friendly kiss of comfort. I couldn't bear that. If he ever kisses me again I want it to be for real—a lover's kiss.

He made no attempt to kiss her. 'That's better,' he said after a moment, dropping his hands. 'Now you have some colour in your cheeks. But what you really need is some fresh air. Let's walk down to the pub and have a drink and a bite to eat. It'll do you good to have a change of scene.'

The unexpectedness of the invitation made her heart pump jerkily. There was nothing she would like better than to spend an evening in his company but did she dare? Could she hide her newly discovered overwhelming. love for him? She would have to learn to do so on duty but socially, no it would be silly to risk it.

'I can't. I'm in uniform,' she said, unable to think of anything else to say, knowing it was a feeble excuse and conscious that he knew it was just that.

He gave a rumble of laughter. 'You could change.' His brilliant blue eyes twinkled. 'I'm not planning to abduct you on the spot.'

'I'm tired. I'm going to have a meal in the dining-room and go to bed. . .'

'With a good book,' he interrupted.

'Yes.'

'*Not* a good idea,' he said emphatically. 'You'll just lie there worrying about Gillian Hallett and all the other problems of the day. Do you much more good to come down to the pub and relax, tuck into Bob's pie and chips and then walk off the cholesterol trudging back up the drive in the moonlight.'

Relax—with him and the moonlight? Fat

chance, she thought wryly. But he was right. If she didn't go out she would lie in bed and think. Not about the patients, as he'd suggested, but about how she was going to face life day after day loving him but never being able to declare her love. Could she manage it or would she have to leave Richmond Place and put space between herself and Josh for ever?

The idea chilled her to the bone. She suppressed a shiver. It was something that she would have to think about long and hard but not now. She reached a decision. To hell with the future and what she might or might not do. Tonight she would submerge her feelings, soak up his presence and just enjoy being with him. Surely she had the guts to manage that!

'Well?' he asked, raising a quizzical eyebrow. 'Going to risk a wild night out, carousing at the local?'

She swallowed and took a deep breath. 'Yes,' she said gaily. 'Why not?'

'Why not, indeed.' Josh's mouth quivered and his eyes teased her gently as if he knew the effort she had made to sound carefree. 'Good decision. Meet you here. Give you ten minutes to change.'

'Twenty minutes.'

'Fifteen.'

'All right.'

The silly, meaningless exchange had lightened the mood and smoothed away her reservations. It would be possible to be at ease with him—to put on an act. They smiled at each other as they parted, Phoebe to make her way back upstairs and Josh to stride away across the reception hall to his private office.

It seemed a point of honour to make it within the fifteen minutes that he had stipulated but when she walked slowly down the stairs dead on time she found Josh already there in the hall, talking to Gordon the night porter.

She had mused over what to wear while whisking in and out of the shower—something cool and classic, she thought. And by the time she had finished showering and spraying herself all over with her favourite expensive body perfume, she had decided. She would wear her hip-hugging, wide-bottomed, white linen trousers that enhanced her long legs and a pale lemon silk shirt unbuttoned at the neck and neatly cuffed at the elbow and tucked into her slender waistband.

Conscious that she felt, looked and smelt good, she walked tall like a model. The pale outfit suited her, contrasting dramatically with her short-cropped mahogany hair, heavily fringed dark brown eyes and lightly tanned skin. She wanted Josh to approve but didn't want to send out false signals or give herself away. Tall order!

His eyes told her that he *did* approve as he walked across the gleaming polished floor to meet her when she reached the foot of the stairs. His frankly admiring blue gaze swept her from shining head to opened-toed, flat-heeled sandals and her heart beat a little tattoo.

'My dear Phoebe, you *do* look nice,' he murmured. 'Super—just right for a summer's evening in a country pub.'

'Thank you.' She thought that he looked super, too, in a navy blue, open-necked knitted cotton shirt that moulded itself to his broad chest and wide shoulders, tucked into pleated, well-cut, lightweight moleskin trousers. Definitely designer gear. A tangle of crisp tawny curls matching his hair and beard filled the V at his throat.

He touched her hand. 'Come on,' he urged

in a surprisingly gruff voice, 'let's go. I'm dying for a pint of Bob's real ale. It's been one hell of a strange day, what with Fliss and the storm and so on.'

Silently she agreed. It had been a strange day. He nodded goodbye to Gordon and, placing a large hand on the small of her back which sent ripples up her spine, steered her before him out into the soft radiance of the blue and gold and purple of the late June evening.

Except that there was a freshness in the air there was no sign of the storm that had raged that afternoon.

There were several people strolling on the lawns or sitting on the terrace beneath striped umbrellas. Tonight, thought Phoebe, in spite of the wheelchairs and the crutches and nurses and carers in uniform, Richmond Place looked more of a country house hotel than a convalescent home.

They exchanged pleasantries with patients and staff nearby as they crossed the terrace to the broad sweep of the gravel concourse in front of the house. The herbaceous beds bordering the concourse smelt delicious, a heady pot-pourri of the scent of roses, stocks, honeysuckle and madonna lilies, mixed with the aromatic earthy smell that follows rain.

They didn't talk at first but meandered slowly down the drive, unwinding, both thinking their own thoughts and not wanting to break the silence that drifted gossamer-like between them—not dividing them but drawing them together.

Phoebe bubbled with quiet happiness. Everything seemed so right. They were so at ease with each other that she had to remind herself of the secret she had to keep, knowing that he must never guess at her true feelings. He was being kind and looking out for one of his staff—nothing more. But she couldn't deny the empathy flowing between them. His heart might not be involved the way hers was but he was drawn to her, there was no denying that.

The bubble of happiness swelled in her breast. Just to be with him for tonight was enough. Make the most of it, she told herself, tomorrow could take care of itself. It would be back to being doctor and nurse.

She glanced across at him and found that he was looking at her, eyes gleaming and a small smile tugging at his lips. He reached out and took her hand. 'You look happier now,' he said softly.

'I am.'

Still holding hands, they reached the humpback bridge and paused at the top of the hump to lean over the parapet and stare down at the crystal-clear, fast-running stream.

Phoebe was fascinated by its effervescent clarity. 'Doesn't it ever dry up?' she asked. 'Even in summer in hot weather?'

'No, it's fed by an underground spring that seems unstoppable.'

'It's so cool and beautiful.'

Josh said huskily, 'Just like you, Phoebe, cool and beautiful.' He squeezed her hand and glanced sideways at her.

She was conscious that he was looking at her and her heart thudded so hard that she thought he must hear it. He had called her beautiful. Did he mean it or was it just an empty compliment, the sort of compliment that Neil used to pay almost automatically to women? How should she react—treat it lightly or seriously?

Except for the flutter and trilling of birds and the humming of insects in the willow trees overhanging the stream, there was a golden silence all around them. Her mind raced as she continued to stare down into the water.

The silence lengthened. How could she respond without giving herself away? One thing was sure, she couldn't remain drooping over the bridge for ever. She would have to face Josh sooner or later. Slowly she lifted her head and turned to look at him and at that moment a car came into view, cruising slowly down the drive from the direction of the house.

The distraction couldn't have come at a better moment and Phoebe gave a little sigh of relief and made to pull her hand from Josh's but he continued to grasp it firmly.

The car, which Phoebe recognised as belonging to Jim Walker—one of the physiotherapists—pulled up beside them. He leaned out of the window and gave them a mischievous, suggestive smile. 'Hello, folks, want a lift down to the village?' he asked.

'No, thanks,' replied Josh. 'We're enjoying the walk after being cooped up all day.'

'Fair enough,' Jim said. 'Just thought I'd offer. Goodnight. See you tomorrow.' He saluted and accelerated away.

'Oh, Lord, it would be him,' said Phoebe. 'He's a terrible gossip.'

'So?'

Phoebe felt the colour mounting in her cheeks. 'It'll be all round the house that we were together and—well—holding hands.'

Josh stared at her for a moment, his eyes twinkling like mad, then tilted back his head and gave a bellow of laughter. 'And you *mind*,' he said in an astonished voice. 'Afraid you'll lose your reputation?'

Phoebe tugged hard and this time succeeded in pulling her hand from his. 'Of course *I* don't mind,' she said, 'but I thought you might.'

'Me? Why, for heaven's sake? It's not criminal to hold a woman's hand in this day and age, is it? Surely even the grapevine can't make anything of that, can they?' He sounded genuinely perplexed. 'Holding hands! Or is that classed as sexual harassment these days?' His eyes quizzed her.

She shook her head and gave an uncertain little laugh. 'No, of course not, but. . .' Her voice trailed off. She really didn't know what to say or how to explain.

'But?' he persisted. He wasn't going to let her off the hook.

'It's going to cause quite a stir for *you* to be seen holding hands with me or anyone else for that matter. Just walking casually down the drive together is one thing but holding hands is something else. It's just something that *you*, as the boss, never do. You don't hold hands and you don't date women.'

As she spoke she felt suddenly raw. Why had he asked her out? Her earlier euphoria drained away, it had all been in her imagination, the empathy she had felt flowing between them— she had deceived herself.

'But I'm dating you now,' he said quietly.

Phoebe shook her head slowly. 'No,' she said sadly as the truth dawned on her. 'You're not really dating me, not in the accepted sense. You're treating me just as you would a patient; you're giving me therapy. You could see that I was upset and you wanted to help as you always do. I'm just another one of your lame ducks to be put back on my feet.'

He gave her a long, hard look and said tersely, 'Not true.' He paused. 'Well, partially true. Of course I could see that you were distressed and

I wanted to help but I asked you out to the pub because *I* wanted your company.'

'I don't believe you,' she said flatly.

'Why not?'

'Because you don't need me. You don't seem to need anybody. You're too self-sufficient— your work is all you care about.'

'Rubbish,' he ground out explosively. 'Everyone needs someone and I'm not immune to that need.'

He sounded absolutely genuine. 'Aren't you?' she said uncertainly.

'No.'

'But what about. . .?' She lost her nerve and couldn't say it.

His firm mouth curled at the corners. 'My famous, disastrous love affair that turned me against women? You've been listening to too much gossip, Phoebe,' he said harshly. 'That was a long time ago. It's over and done with.'

She said hesitantly, 'Is it, Josh? You some-times look so sad as if you were remembering.'

'Do I? I thought I was seen to be totally in control of my feelings. The untouchable Dr Richmond—great at solving other people's problems and past master at concealing my own.' He sounded bitter. He turned his head away for a moment and stared down into the water.

When he turned back he found himself looking into her soft, brown, gold-flecked eyes. Eyes full of tenderness and compassion. Her wide, generous mouth looked soft, too, and her red lips moist and vulnerable.

He wanted to kiss her, he acknowledged to himself. Not in an avuncular fashion as he had during the thunderstorm that afternoon but with a normal, healthy, sexual passion. He'd had enough of his monkish existence. For the past few weeks this lovely woman, this admirable nurse, had been getting under his skin and, though he was loath to admit it, subtly eroding the barriers he'd erected.

Phoebe made herself return his look steadily. 'That is the impression that you give most of the time—that you are remote and controlled—but I have sometimes wondered.'

'Have you?'

'Yes.'

He moved along the parapet, closing the small gap between them. Their shoulders touched. He felt her quiver, saw her eyes darken and was conscious that she was acutely aware of him. 'You're very percipient,' he said huskily.

'But I haven't got your shadow sight.'

'But you do know that I want to kiss you.'

'Yes, but that's just female intuition.'

'Do you *want* me to kiss you?' His instinct told him that she did but he needed to hear her say so. She was vulnerable. She had been hurt—he didn't know how but it was a fact—and he wasn't going to add to the hurt, much as he wanted physical contact with her.

'Yes,' she breathed, knowing that she shouldn't let him near her for fear that she might give herself away but at that moment not caring. He wanted a kiss, a simple kiss. It was no big deal—he didn't have to know that it meant more than that to her. All common sense fled. She longed to feel his arms about her and longed to feel his lips on hers. He didn't have to know that her heart was involved.

He glanced casually up and down the drive. It was empty. He cupped her face in his hands and bent his leonine head, shining gold in the late evening sunlight, over her until his mouth met hers. His lips brushed against her lips in little sweeping movements as he turned his head from side to side, his nose rubbing gently against her nose and his silky beard whispering against her chin softly and sensuously.

Then his mouth opened and settled over hers and his tongue made little darting movements against her lips until they parted and his tongue slid easily into the moist softness within.

She couldn't resist him: she lifted her arms and tangled her hands in his thick mane of hair, imprisoning his head. Slowly he dropped his hands from her face and slid them down her back and over the neat curve of her buttocks, pulling her close until their hips and thighs touched and she felt him hard with desire, with physical hunger, and she knew that it must have been a long time since he'd held a woman this close.

Time stood still as she stood within the circle of his arms. He wants me, she thought exultantly, he wants me. But he doesn't love you, whispered a small detached voice in her head. He only wants you as Neil wanted you, just for sex. He's in love with that other woman, the one who jilted him.

She had thought that it wouldn't matter that he didn't love her; that just to feel him close would be enough. But it wasn't enough. Abruptly she disentangled her hands from his hair and jerked her mouth from his.

He lifted his head. 'What's wrong?' he asked sharply.

'A car. I thought I heard another car coming.'

His eyebrows shot up. 'No, there's no car,' he said drily and she knew that he had seen through her invention.

She blushed and then paled. He looked down at her, his bright, intelligent eyes seeming to pierce right through her. 'But you're scared, aren't you? That's why you pulled away from me. I rushed things—raised ghosts from the past. I should have known better and restrained myself. You wanted to be kissed. You wanted more than a chaste kiss to prove to yourself that you are still an attractive woman—to restore your self-respect—but the last thing you wanted was a sex-starved man hassling you.'

'How do you know that?' she whispered.

'Because I know something of rejection by someone you love and sex alone is no replacement. The trauma goes deeper than that. Believe me, there's a lot of it about—rejection of one sort or another.'

Was he speaking personally or in his role as a counsellor? Was he still hopelessly in love with the woman who had jilted him or had he come to terms with it? He had said that it had finished a long time ago but then why did he sometimes look so sad, so bleak, as if haunted by a bad memory? Dared she ask?

He didn't give her a chance. He took her hands in his and squeezed them gently. 'Forget the over-the-top kiss,' he said in a calm, even voice. 'Let's be friends. We both have a void to fill and we both need a friend, a special friend. I'm not a natural celibate—' he gave her a lop-sided grin '—as perhaps you noticed but unless *you* want it I promise no sex or entanglements of any sort—just plain unvarnished friendship, companionship, going out together as friends do. Are you game?'

Game! Was she game? Could she put on an act and pretend to friendship when she wanted so much more? She stared into his eyes, smoky blue now and no longer piercing. How quickly they'd changed! At least he didn't seem to suspect that she was deeply in love with him—that was a plus—and he wasn't pretending that he was in love with her—that was another plus.

He was being honest. And what was the alternative to friendship? Leaving Richmond Place. Going away and trying to forget him, leaving him for ever.

She couldn't do it. The thought of never seeing him again, never hearing his rich deep voice and never watching his clever hands tending a patient, made her feel hollow and sick. Life would be meaningless, lonely beyond belief.

Somehow she had to find the courage to be with him day after day and pretend to friendship when she wanted love. Other women had done it. She could do it. It was a common phenomenon, wasn't it, that secretaries fell in love with their bosses and nurses with doctors? From somewhere deep inside her she dredged up a smile and, continuing to look boldly into his eyes, said softly but firmly, 'Yes, Josh, I'm game.'

'Great.' He kissed her on both cheeks and smiled down at her, his eyes teasing. 'Now if the rumours start, as you seem to think they will, you can honestly say that we're *just good friends*.' He paused and, suddenly serious, added, 'The very best of friends.'

* * *

But would anyone believe that they were just friends? Phoebe wondered the following morning as, bracing herself to face the day and whatever it threw at her, she went on duty. She had a job to believe it herself, loving him as she did. Could she possibly keep up this pretence of friendship in the face of suggestive gossip? She knew, nobody better, what a hospital grapevine could do and the way it could enhance and embroider stories just like the tabloid press.

Josh had no such hang-ups. He had been his usual confident and reassuring self as they'd continued their walk down the drive as the sun had begun to sink low in the west. And when they'd reached the ancient, timbered, black and white pub he had wished everyone a cheerful good evening and, oblivious to the sideways looks they'd been receiving, had found them a secluded corner. When their drinks had arrived he'd touched her glass with his and murmured, 'To friendship,' and she had sipped her drink and had softly repeated his toast.

It was clear from early in the day that Jim Walker's tongue and others' had already been busy.

By mid-morning it was common knowledge

that Phoebe and Josh had been walking hand in hand down the drive and had spent the evening together in the Richmond Arms. There had been plenty of witnesses to that as the pub had been full of off-duty staff and a number of holidaying residents.

Not that anyone had been surprised when she and Josh had first arrived. It was not unusual for Josh to call in for a drink and Phoebe, like everyone else at Richmond Place, used the pub as her local.

Curiosity had been roused when Josh had steered her to a secluded corner and had been enhanced later when it had been learned that they had been holding hands in what Jim, with a leer, had described as a 'meaningful manner'. Tongues had then started wagging.

Phoebe, busy in the dispensary giving injections, changing dressings, taking bloods, syringing ears, putting drops in eyes and carrying out a dozen other small nursing tasks, wondered if Josh was aware of the rumours.

When, a little later, she joined him in his consulting-room she could see by his face that he was. He grinned at her across the desk and her heart turned over. 'Well, have they got us married off yet?'

'Almost.' Her voice was steady. She smiled wryly. 'But I can't imagine why. They know we haven't been going out together and that I haven't been here long. It's incredible. You're much fancied, you know, a lone, eligible bachelor. I hope they won't think I've muscled in on their territory.'

'They won't,' he said confidently. 'Everyone's been trying to get me paired off for a long time and has given me up as a lost cause. I think they'll be quite pleased to find that I'm as vulnerable as the next man.'

'Even if we *are* just good friends?'

'Even so. Don't worry, Phoebe, it'll be a storm in a teacup, as Granny would say. It'll blow over in no time. People will read into it what they want to and we'll probably end up by being an item, a twosome. But we can live with that, can't we, for friendship's sake?' He raised a questioning eyebrow and smiled his heart-stopping, lopsided smile and she remembered how gentle and understanding he had been on the bridge last night.

A twosome. No longer alone. It sounded

great. He was not in love with her as she was with him but he was offering her the next best thing—true friendship—and sex if and when she wanted it. That was something worth cherishing, if she had the nerve and could preserve her secret.

She returned his smile, the golden flecks in her warm brown eyes glowing. 'Yes,' she said softly, 'I guess we can live with that, for friendship's sake.'

CHAPTER SEVEN

To Phoebe's relief, gossip and speculation about them was mostly good-natured and teasing rather than malicious.

There had, of course, been a few snide remarks from some people but they were silly rather than hurtful. Fran Fielding, one of her nursing colleagues, divorced and known to be on the look-out for a replacement partner and who at one time had had a predatory eye on Josh, made some veiled, rather shrewish, comments about pushy newcomers making a play for the boss for his money and position and to further their own advancement. But hers was the only really unkind reaction.

Well, I can live with the bitchy Fran Fielding, thought Phoebe, nobody else seems to resent the fact that Josh is friendly towards me. They've all been great about it.

It was easy to reassure herself that she wasn't going to lose the goodwill of her colleagues but less easy to come to terms with loving Josh and having to hide it.

Standing on the humpback bridge in the soft evening sunshine and knowing he wasn't in love with her in spite of the passionate, fevered kiss they had just exchanged, it had seemed possible to commit herself to a lasting, precious friendship.

But as the days passed she began to realise just how hard it was going to be to keep up the charade. It was a sort of agony, as well as ecstasy, to be with him, near him, and yet be afraid to touch him with any degree of intimacy or confide in him as friends might. She longed to do both and yet she dared not do either for fear that she would give herself away.

She could be detached and superficially friendly when they were on duty—they were busy and she was used to suppressing her personal feelings and getting on with the job—but off duty was a different matter. It was an effort to be casually friendly when he joined the staff table for a meal and sat beside her or partnered her in a game of darts or snooker in the club room.

It was unnerving to find herself having to

fight to remain calm and collected in his presence. It was hard to look him in the eye or accidentally touch him or be touched by him without blushing or trembling as the sheer masculine power that he generated coursed through her like an electric shock. She loved the look of him and the tangy, male smell of him. She had never been so affected before by any man, not even Neil at the zenith of their affair.

I'm like a schoolgirl with a hopeless crush, she berated herself derisively, and I've got to damn well pull myself together.

But as the days following the bridge episode slipped by she felt that she was living on a knife-edge, always afraid of giving herself away, yet wanting to be near him. It was hell. If love hurt one-sided love hurt more.

Not that she blamed him for not being in love with her. He hadn't professed to more than friendship, however special he wanted that to be. And, except on rare occasions, he was a reserved man, not given to displaying his feelings unless a patient needed warmth and reassurance and then he gave it in abundance.

But, in spite of this reserve, in front of other staff when off duty he made no secret of the fact that he enjoyed her company, innocently adding fuel to the fire of the rumour that there was something romantic between them.

If they only knew, she thought sadly. As far as Josh was concerned it was a relationship based on a special friendship with a casual side-offering of sex thrown in and she would have to accept those terms or reject them by leaving Richmond Place because love didn't figure in Josh's offer.

But when Maeve, returning from days off, showed no surprise on learning through the grapevine that she and Josh were being linked together the faint possibility that she might be wrong about that sent a frisson of hope trickling through her.

They met up in the dispensary and Maeve said gleefully, her green eyes brimming with laughter, 'What's all this I hear about you and the boss?'

Phoebe groaned. 'A lot of exaggerated nonsense,' she said flatly.

'Oh, I think not,' said Maeve. 'It was obvious that there was something going on between you two right from the start so I'm not surprised to learn that you've been holding hands with the gorgeous man himself as soon as my back's turned. God knows what you will be up to next—such goings-on,' she teased.

What did Maeve mean, something going on right from the start? What does she know that I don't? Her heart thumped wildly against her chest wall. She said vehemently, 'Look, let me put things straight. There's *nothing* going on between us. We happened to come off duty together one evening and he invited me for a drink and a meal at the local, that's all.

'We'd had a pretty hectic afternoon with poor Fliss Brownlow bleeding like a stuck pig from a spontaneous rupture of her long saphenous and I got a bit uptight after visiting Gillian Hallett and trying to counsel her for the first time. Josh simply took pity on me, that was all, and we walked down to the pub together.'

'Stuff! Took pity on you! It's crystal clear from the way he looks at you when he thinks that other people won't notice that he fancies you rotten.'

Phoebe swallowed and her heart thumped even louder and faster. What did Maeve mean, he 'fancies me'? She said in a cool, rather amused tone, 'If only.' She pulled a wry face.

'What a crude expression—"fancies me".'

'And *you* fancy him like mad,' said Maeve in a flat, suddenly serious voice, ignoring the caustic comment.

Phoebe laughed and shrugged. Maeve seemed to see right through her. That's all I need, she thought, another Celt with shadow sight. 'Doesn't everyone?' she said lightly. 'Well, anyway, all the females at Richmond Place— after all, he's our most eligible bachelor.'

'True!' Maeve smiled, a knowing smile, and said softly, 'But we *only* fancy him. It's a bit of a game and we know he's unobtainable, whereas you. . . Admit it, old thing, you're seriously nuts about the man.'

For one fleeting moment Phoebe considered baring her heart to her friend, who already seemed to know so much, but the moment passed. There was no way that she could tell Maeve what had happened on the bridge or confide to her the depths of her feelings for Josh. It would somehow feel like a betrayal of him, of their pact of friendship. 'And *I* only *fancy* him, too, to use your revolting phrase,' she said repressively. 'And, for the record, to use that corny old line, we're just good friends.'

'There's friendship and friendship,' replied Maeve enigmatically, 'and it's the best foundation for any relationship, romantic or otherwise. Now I'm away to do a room round. You go and help the boss with the clinic and admission examinations.' She grinned cheekily. 'Working in close proximity all the morning, you'll both enjoy that.'

It'll be like walking through a minefield, thought Phoebe, trying not to give myself away, wondering if Maeve's right and he does. . . She switched off her thoughts and said with pretended hauteur, 'I always enjoy my work, Staff Nurse Connelly, with or without the boss.'

'Of course you do,' agreed Maeve. 'But you must admit, love, that having him around is a bonus.' She looked at her fob-watch. 'And you'd better scoot if you don't want to keep the great man waiting,' she added with a laugh as she left the dispensary.

'Wouldn't dare,' said Phoebe, pulling a face at her retreating back as she followed Maeve out and made her way next door to the surgery suite.

She spent a few minutes in the ante-room collecting patients' files as she made a determined effort to put her conversation with Maeve

out of her mind before knocking on the consulting-room door. Josh's deep voice called to
her to enter. He was in the middle of a phone
call but his firm lips curved into a wide, welcoming smile when he saw her and her heart
gave a little leap of joy at the warmth of
that smile.

His eyes smiled too as they met hers briefly
and he waved her into the chair opposite him.
'Won't be long,' he mouthed, his hand over the
mouthpiece. He turned his attention back to
what was being said by the caller and glanced
down at some papers on his desk.

Pretending to look at the files she had collected, Phoebe studied him through lowered
lashes. Not that she needed to study him for
she knew every bone and muscle of his
handsome face.

She knew to a hair how his thick, tawny mane
sprang from his high forehead and tapered into
the nape of his neck just above his collar and
how closely the neatly trimmed beard outlined
his firm jaw. She knew how the nostrils of his
aquiline nose would sometimes flare with otherwise concealed anger and how his thick brows
came together in a frown of concentration.

He was frowning now as he spoke briskly into the phone and made notes on the pad in front of him. But only moments before he had been smiling—smiling at me, she thought, staring down unseeingly at the file on her lap— a wonderful smile, a tender smile. . .

So was Maeve right when she said that he 'fancied her rotten' and even implied that it was more than that and he was seriously attracted to her? Was it possible? Were his deeper feelings involved and had he been speaking the truth when he'd said that his abortive love affair was behind him? Supposing that he was not just interested in sex, as she had suspected. Supposing the special friendship that he'd suggested was a smoke-screen to conceal his true feelings. . .

Josh's voice crashed in on her thoughts. He was speaking to her. He had finished his phone call and was looking hard at her, his eyes very blue, amused, gentle. She blinked at him. 'So sorry,' she murmured. 'I. . . I. . .' Her voice trailed off, the files slipped from her lap to the floor and she stared down at them helplessly, unable to move.

'You were miles away,' he said softly, standing up and moving round the desk. He crouched down in front of her and began gathering up the folders.

The longing to put out a hand and stroke his hair was overwhelming but she stopped herself and, instead, slid to the floor beside him and began collecting up the loose leaves that lay scattered everywhere. To her horror she saw that her hands were shaking slightly. She prayed that he wouldn't notice. The phone rang and he muttered an expletive. She was relieved. She scrabbled about picking up the last few sheets still on the floor.

'Can you manage?' he asked, standing up and thrusting a bundle of papers at her.

'Yes. I'll take them outside and sort them in the office.'

'Are you sure you're all right?' He looked at her with such curious intensity that she felt herself blushing. His eyes seemed to bore right through her. He wasn't talking about the papers—had he noticed her trembling hands? Had he read her mind when she had been so deep in thought?

She nodded dumbly. 'Fine.'

'Good, we'll make a start as soon as I've

taken this call.' He moved back round the desk and picked up the phone. 'Josh Richmond,' he said in a gravelly sort of voice and Phoebe was aware of his eyes following her as she left the room and quietly closed the door behind her.

She paused briefly in the ante-room to put the files in order and do what she always did when personal matters threatened to impinge on her professional persona. She closed her eyes, took a deep breath, squashed her tattered thoughts and prepared to do her duty by her patients.

Did Josh have a similar formula, she wondered, to separate his professional life from his personal life? In front of patients she had never seen him anything but calm and in control but in private she had known him to be coldly angry as at the accident on the day she had met him and fervently aroused as when he had taken her into his arms on the bridge.

He was capable of giving way to his feelings so maybe the intense but silent exchange that had just taken place between them had been significant to him. Would he have said or done something revealing had the telephone not rung?

Irritably she squashed the question, which

was unlikely to be answered. And he gave no clue to his feelings when a little later he buzzed for his first patient—for he was his usual pleasant, professional self.

Most of the patients for the general clinic that morning were convalescents booked to see him for a final check-up before going home. With her usual efficiency Phoebe removed dressings for him to examine healing wounds, collected prescribed medication from the dispensary, gave injections and filled in discharge certificates for Josh to sign.

His last patient was Lucy Harris, a pretty young woman of nineteen who, in spite of suffering the sometimes excruciating pain of rheumatoid arthritis, managed to be incredibly cheerful.

She said seriously, as Phoebe helped her to struggle back into her clothes after Josh had given her a thorough examination and proclaimed her fit to go home. 'I'm really grateful, Doctor, to you and the staff. I think you're all brilliant. What with my arthritis and the accident and dislocating my shoulder there was no way I could have managed at home, even with Mum's help, when I first left hospital. It's been a life saver coming here.

'And the physio and massage and swimming have been great. And meeting people of my own age with all sorts of disabilities has been great too. I don't feel such a freak as I used to.'

'Lucy, my dear girl, you're no freak; you're incredibly well adjusted—' Josh bent over her wheelchair and gently patted her swollen, distorted hands '—but I do know what you mean about mixing with people of your own age with similar limitations. You don't feel so alone. Keep in touch with them, Lucy. Many of them live within range of Heresham.

'Why don't you form a club and have regular meetings? Perhaps we could arrange for you to use some of the facilities here on occasion.'

Lucy's eyes sparkled. 'Would that really be possible?'

'I don't see why not,' said Josh. 'I've been mulling over the idea for providing a post-convalescent service for some time. This area's short on activities for young people, especially the young disabled. Keep me informed about the way things go and we'll talk about it but it'll be up to you to set the ball rolling.'

Lucy beamed. 'Thanks, Doc, I'll do that. It'll keep me out of mischief. You're a gem.' She kissed her fingertips and reached up and touched his face and ran her fingers along his jaw. 'Love the beard,' she said with a cheeky grin. 'Very sexy.'

Two thoughts struck Phoebe one, that, astonishingly, she also loved his beard; and two, that Lucy had overstepped the mark by being too free with him, too intimate. Surely Josh would recoil at such intimacy.

But she was wrong. He seemed not to mind in the least for he gave a bark of laughter and bent and kissed Lucy on both cheeks. 'You're a forward wee lassie, as my grandmother would say,' he rumbled, 'and I should report you for sexual harassment.'

'And you'd be dead right and I wouldn't even try to defend myself,' laughed Lucy. She pressed a button on the arm of her wheelchair and swivelled round to face the door. 'Anyway, I'm off now but I'll be seeing you and, again, thanks for everything, Dr Richmond,' she said in a quiet, suddenly formal voice, as she propelled herself smoothly across the room.

Phoebe held the door open for her and bent

to kiss her cheek. 'Goodbye, Lucy. You've been a super patient. Look after yourself and take care.'

'Will do. And you take care too, Phoebe, you're a cracker of a nurse.' As she manoeuvred herself skilfully through the doorway she glanced slyly up, winked and murmured, 'And take care of the boss—he's a fabulous doctor and a lovely man.'

Yes, he's all of that, thought Phoebe, closing the door slowly as Lucy wended her way through the waiting-room. He deserves all the praise that's been dished out to him this morning by the departing patients.

She felt a flush of vicarious pride in his skill, dedication and charisma and was immensely pleased that it was acknowledged and appreciated by those he cared for. Happy that he inspired such genuine, uninhibited affection.

With all her heart she wished that she could be as easygoing with him as Lucy had been but she couldn't be—she would give herself away if she touched him as Lucy had touched him. Hell, she nearly had done so earlier when she'd tried to gather up the files and her hands had shaken in that ridiculous fashion.

But if he was attracted to her, as Maeve had suggested, did it matter? That was unanswerable! It was pathetic—just to be near him did strange things to her, as if she were a teenager in love for the first time. But isn't that just what I am—*really* in love for the first time in twenty-six years? she mused.

'Day-dreaming again, Phoebe?' For the second time that morning Josh's voice cut in on her thoughts.

Was he being sarcastic? 'Sorry.' She forced a smile to her lips and turned to face him.

No, he wasn't being sarcastic because he asked in an incredibly gentle voice, 'Is anything wrong? You don't seem yourself this morning.' His eyes met hers across the width of the room. It was as if he were looking into her heart and mind and reading her like a book.

Nonsense, he couldn't be that telepathic for all his shadow sight. She moistened her lips with the tip of her tongue and smiled again. 'No, nothing's wrong,' she said brightly. 'Bit of a headache, that's all.'

His eyes glinted and he raised one eyebrow. 'Really! I'm glad it's nothing worse.' His voice was dry, disbelieving. 'Not bad enough to stop you coming out tonight for a meal?'

She could cope with that, just. The usual crowd would be down in the village. 'I'd like that. I like Bob's pub grub.'

He grinned. 'Oh, I was thinking of something rather more exotic than the local. Somewhere further afield where we can get together, just the two of us, and enjoy each other's company without an interested audience. Considering we're such good friends we haven't done much socialising. It's time we talked together, Phoebe, just the two of us.'

Involuntarily she put a hand up to her throat. 'Oh, but I can't. I. . .not just us. . .alone. . .' Her voice wobbled to a halt. She knew she sounded scared—she *was* scared. Scared of giving herself away, scared that she would say too much and reveal too much about herself and the past.

Josh raised an eyebrow like a question mark. 'But what, Phoebe? Why are you so afraid of being alone with me, talking to me? I just want to move our relationship forward. Just talk— nothing more.'

'You—you promised that you wouldn't press me about my past. You said that you'd wait till I was ready but all you want to do is analyse me, like any other patient. It's not damn well fair nor professional to do that.' Her voice was a bit uneven, a bit shrill, but she walked with firm steps across the room and stood boldly in front of him. She lifted her chin and stared him straight in the eye.

'I would never have believed it of you, Josh. I thought you were a man of honour.'

Josh brought his thick eyebrows together in a frown and he stared at her in amazement. He put his hands on her shoulders and squeezed them hard.

'My dear Phoebe, who the devil said anything about digging into your past? I can't pretend that I'm not interested in it—we're supposed to be good friends, remember? And I want to help if I can. But no way would I pressurise you into telling me anything that you don't want to.' His eyes bored into hers.

He shrugged. 'I just thought it would be pleasant to have an evening out together away from this place and our colleagues and work so that we could both relax and enjoy each other's company but it seems I was wrong. Pity!' His eyes looked suddenly cold and hard. He gave her a little shake.

'Are you rejecting our friendship? Are you always going to shy away from me? Do you want to leave Richmond Place? Did you really think that I was asking you out so that I could pump you?'

Gone was his usual cool. He was an angry man. His nostrils flared. The questions came out like pistol shots. Phoebe would have taken a step back but Josh still held her firmly, his hands burning through the thin cotton of her uniform dress to her shoulders. She was appalled by the mixture of contempt and fury in his eyes. How could she have accused him of behaving badly, unprofessionally? How could she have been so stupid?

Her respirations were fast and shallow and her chest hurt as if she had been running a marathon. She said breathlessly, 'Of course I'm not rejecting our friendship, Josh, and I don't want to leave here and it was ridiculous of me to suggest that you wanted to pump me. I know that you wouldn't do a thing like that. Please forgive me,' and, amazed at her own nerve, she lifted her hand and laid it against his cheek in a pleading sort of gesture. 'And I don't *want* to shy away from you. I'm just afraid of. . .'

He clasped the wrist of her raised hand. 'Afraid of what?' he ground out between clenched teeth.

Dared she tell him the truth—that she loved him and was afraid of revealing it? Of course not—better a half-truth. 'Of getting too close to you—too fond of you—spoiling our friendship and asking too much of you. Please understand, Josh, please.'

Some of the anger faded from his smouldering eyes, though they continued to burn into hers with a frightening intensity. His clasp on her wrist tightened. His mouth was a straight line, his eyebrows still beetling. In a low, harsh voice he grated, 'You want me to understand—to forgive you—but you don't trust me, do you, Phoebe?'

'I do. Of course I do.'

'But not enough to tell me the truth, the whole truth.'

A sudden rage shafted through her. What more did he want from her? She had apologised, practically grovelled. She wouldn't tell him that she loved him. She wouldn't. Let him find out for himself with his precious shadow sight just how much she loved him and if he had any deep feelings for her let him say so; let him put himself on the line.

She tried to pull her hand away from his. 'Do you mind?' Her voice was icy.

'Well, actually, I do,' he said mockingly. He gave what she could only interpret as a grim, almost cruel smile, his lips barely quirking at the corners as his eyes slid over her from top to toe and back. 'I'd like to be holding more than your hand and I'm damn well sure that that's what you would like too. Aren't I right?'

His eyes blazed arrogantly into hers. He hadn't forgiven her for doubting his honour. The gentle Dr Richmond had metamorphosed into the dominant macho male. Even his mane of tawny hair and matching beard seemed stronger and wirier, springing more vibrantly from scalp and jaw. His shoulders seemed broader, his muscles tense. The marauding Viking of her dreams. She had never seen him like this. He both frightened and excited her at one and the same time.

She shivered as, at arm's length, his eyes challenged her. She felt naked and exposed to his gaze but she lifted her chin still higher in defiance and spat out, 'That's for you to find out, Josh. The ball's in your court.'

He inclined his head slightly in a parody of a bow. 'Good, then come out to dinner with me tonight and we'll get the ball into play. I'll pick you up at eight sharp.' Abruptly he let go of her wrist and her arm fell heavily to her side. He moved back round the desk, sat down and opened a folder.

'Now, let's get cracking on these admissions. I'll see the cystic fibrosis twins first if you round them up. Nice kids. They were here last year after a bad bout of bronchiectasis, whilst their parents had a break, so they know the drill.'

Phoebe simmered with fury as she stared down at the top of his head. How dared he revert so calmly, so quickly, from aggressive man to caring doctor? He was like a chameleon. Ruthlessly she thrust down her own boiling emotions and marched across to the door. 'I'll have them here in a few minutes,' she said in an expressionless voice. 'I thought you would want to see them first so I arranged for them to stay in their room till you sent for them.'

'Efficient as always,' he murmured to her stiff back as she whisked through the door and she could *hear* the smile in his voice.

Jason and Mike Smithers, the cystic fibrosis patients, were thin, gangly, sallow-looking youths of seventeen with cropped reddish-brown hair and bright hazel eyes. Josh saw first Jason and then Mike, giving each of them a thorough top to toe examination, paying particular attention to their narrow, bony chests and flat but flaccid abdomens.

'We'll keep you both on the same antibiotics that you're having at present,' he said when they were dressed and sitting opposite him.

'You're both doing well generally and, as your GP says in his letter, your bronchiectasis seems to be under control and has been all winter. But while you're here we'll increase your physiotherapy to three times a day and put you on a high protein and high calorie diet to build you up a bit. And I want you to take plenty of sensible exercise. Join in the various activities but don't get over-tired.'

Their thin faces lit up. 'Can we swim this year?' they asked eagerly in unison.

'As often as you like as long as you don't hang around afterwards and get chilled. Don't want you picking up a cold or any other nasties. Now, off you go and start enjoying yourselves and report to the dispensary this afternoon for your medication and a list of the times for your physio. Staff Nurse Phoebe here will sort you out. Let her know if you have any problems. She'll keep you in order.'

He glanced across at Phoebe, who was tidying the examination couch, caught her eye and smiled—a warm, crooked, humorous yet intimate smile.

Her heart fluttered. Was this an olive branch? Tentatively she smiled back and, somehow, amazingly, the smile put everything right and wiped out the bad vibes that had sparked between them. At that moment there was no need for words. They would come later.

'Brilliant. Will do,' the youths said cheerfully, as they jostled each other through the doorway.

After they'd gone Josh leaned his elbows on the desk and steepled his hands together, pressing them against his chin, and, deep in thought, stared at Phoebe without really seeing her. Speaking almost to himself, he muttered, 'I wonder what the future holds for those two?'

'I thought you were pleased with their progress.'

'Oh, I am. They're doing remarkably well, considering that a few years ago they wouldn't even have reached their seventeenth birthdays, when cystic fibrosis was a childhood killer. But we haven't found a cure yet—only various holding devices and mechanical relief through physio and chemical relief through antibiotics.' He sighed heavily.

'There's so much more to be done, Phoebe, and, as always, not enough time or money.' He pushed long fingers impatiently through his hair.

'But there's hope,' she said softly, 'and there's always research going on.'

He gave her a lopsided grin. 'Yep, you're absolutely right, my dear. There's always research and the hope of a miracle cure just around the corner. Now,' he continued briskly, 'let's have the next patient in.'

Alistair Gibbons had had a successful heart bypass performed eight days earlier and should by now have been making progress but he looked drawn and ill, with shadows under his dark, expressionless eyes and deep lines about his mouth. His thin, bony face was set and he seemed unable to smile.

He was a tall, athletic-looking man of forty. He was not an obvious candidate for a coronary or myocardial infarct but he had, according to his notes, had two over the last few months and the second had nearly been fatal. He was on a range of anti-thrombotic drugs and painkillers and, provided that he kept to a sensible regime of rest, exercise and diet, his prognosis was good.

He sat down stiffly in the easy chair facing the desk.

'Wound sore?' Josh asked.

'Bloody painful but I'm not bothered about that. I dare say it'll pass.'

'In time, when the muscle gets back some tone and the damaged tissues where you've been stitched soften up round the edges, it won't pull so much.'

Mr Gibbons shrugged. 'Doesn't matter. I'll live, unfortunately.' His voice was hard and indifferent.

Josh leaned slightly forward across the desk, his eyes on the man's grim face. '"Unfortunately"? Why "unfortunately", Mr Gibbons?'

'Nothing to live for.'

'Wife, family, friends?'

'Dead! Wife and son dead, killed by a sod-
ding joy-rider too bloody young to prosecute.
So what the hell have I got to live for, Doctor?
You tell me. That's what you're good at, isn't
it, telling the no-hopers like me how to pull
themselves together and get on with life? That's
what they told me at the hospital.' The sneering
bitterness in his voice made Phoebe flinch.

'Then they told you wrongly,' Josh said, his
deep voice very calm and very matter-of-fact,
'or you misinterpreted what they said. All I can
do is listen, if and when you want to talk. It's
up to you, Mr Gibbons. I don't advise and I
certainly don't condemn.'

For a moment the man looked surprised and
then said in a stiff, grudging sort of manner, 'I
might think about it and the name's Alistair.'

Josh nodded and smiled, his eyes kind.
'Right, Alistair, now I want to examine you so
take off your shirt and trousers and hop up on
the couch.'

Phoebe helped him off with his clothes as
both the surgical wound on his chest and the
site on his leg from which the vein for the
bypass had been taken were sore and he looked
fragile enough to pass out, she thought.

It took some time for Josh to examine him, checking his heart, lungs, blood pressure, reflex actions, pulse and temperature and both wound areas. Phoebe, watching and assisting where she could, was, as always, impressed with Josh's thoroughness as he moved his stethoscope steadily over the man's chest and ribcage, listening intently—first to the drumming heartbeats and then to the shallow, uneven respirations.

After a while he straightened up. 'Right, you can get dressed now, old chap, and then we'll have a word about your treatment and the daily regime that I want you to follow.' He moved over to his desk and scribbled busily on the record sheet, while Phoebe helped the breathless patient back into his clothes and sat him in a comfortable armchair.

'Well, your heart's ticking over nicely, Alistair,' Josh said, 'but your lungs are a bit congested so I'm going to give you another antibiotic—and you will be having physio morning and evening to help clear your chest.

'And I want you to take several short walks each day and I do mean ''short'' initially—just along the terrace and across the lawn for the first few days. Then you can be more adventurous. In between your walks you will rest for at least half an hour and more if you need to. And at the end of the week you'll start on a daily exercise programme in the gym.'

He leaned back in his chair and quietly surveyed the bowed head of the man sitting at the other side of the desk.

Alistair lifted his head and stared with dull eyes at Josh. 'Hell-bent on toughening me up and getting me fighting fit again, Doc, aren't you?' He was angry and upset.

Josh nodded. 'That's the general idea,' he said mildly. 'We can do that much for you on the physical side. . .' he let his voice tail off '. . .but if you want any other sort of help, Alistair, it's up to you. You only have to ask.'

'You mean this counselling thing?' he sneered.

'Yes.'

'I might just think about it.'

'Do that. I'm here or on call most of the time. Ask one of the nurses to contact me if you need me.'

Alistair stood up shakily, leaned on the desk and pushed his face almost into Josh's. 'Are you another of those bloody do-gooders?' he growled with a sort of suppressed fury, looking threatening in spite of his fragility.

Phoebe drew in her breath sharply and took an involuntary step towards him.

Josh waved her back and said gently, 'I don't quite know what you mean by that, Alistair. As I explained I'm simply willing to be a friendly listener if that's what you want.'

Alistair continued to stare down at him, swaying a little, unsteady on his feet as if he was drunk. Phoebe moved quickly forward, put an arm round his waist and eased him back into the armchair just as he fainted.

Smoothly, without seeming to hurry, Josh moved round the desk, lifted the man's feet and legs onto another chair and, pulling off his shoes, massaged his ankles and calves until he began to show signs of regaining consciousness.

'You're all right, old boy,' he assured his patient as his eyes flickered open. 'You fainted.' He glanced at Phoebe. 'A spot of brandy and water, I think, Nurse.'

Phoebe poured a small measure from the bottle on the resuscitation tray, always kept at the ready on the examination trolley, and held it to Alistair's bluish lips. He sipped at it greedily and, after a moment, muttered, 'Sorry about that. I'm a bloody fool saying what I did; getting worked up—apologies and all that.'

'You're a sick fool,' said Josh with a nice smile. 'You're still recovering from a serious operation. You've overdone it a bit and are physically and mentally tired. You need to rest. Nurse will take you up to your room in a wheel-chair and see you settled. Stay there for the rest of the day. We'll start your active programme tomorrow, though you'll have some physio this afternoon. Read, watch the telly, listen to the radio and sleep if you can. I'll be up to see you later—before if you need me.'

'Thanks,' said a subdued Alistair as he settled himself into the wheelchair that Phoebe had fetched from the waiting-room. And a little later, as they hummed gently up to the first floor in the elegant lift, he said, 'Rum sort of place this—old-fashioned, not like a hospital—but the doc seems to know his stuff. What do you think, Nurse, is there anything in this counselling lark?'

'It seems to have helped a lot of people,' Phoebe replied cautiously. 'But, as the doctor explained, he doesn't advise or judge—he just listens and helps you listen to yourself.'

'Sort of DIY,' he said, sounding infinitely sad.

'Sort of,' agreed Phoebe, putting a comforting hand on his shoulder and wishing that she could do more. He was so remote and so unhappy. Like Gillian Hallett, she realised, suffering post-traumatic shock following his operation and the death of his wife and baby.

CHAPTER EIGHT

THE surgery was empty when Phoebe arrived back after seeing a sad, weary Alistair to his room and bed. She'd left him propped up against a mound of pillows in the care of June, one of the assistant nurses, who'd told him cheerfully that she would be popping in from time to time but that he was to ring if he wanted anything.

There was a note for her on the desk in Josh's bold hand. It couldn't have been briefer or more to the point:

Phoebe,
Called away. Pick you up tonight as arranged. Wear something pretty—J.

Wear something pretty! The thought carried her through the day as she went about her chores, for once letting her personal feelings drift in and out of her mind as she worked. It was important to him how she looked. The smile they had exchanged following their earlier acrimonious remarks had mattered to him as it had to her.

The confrontation that they'd had had done her good, restored her pride and her courage. She could face him now without being afraid of giving herself away. She glowed. It was going to be a good evening. They would eat and drink and talk and this time she wouldn't shy away from him if the talk became intimate. And if Maeve was right and he did love her... If he did? Wave after wave of joy washed through her. She felt alive, tingling.

'You look different. Effervescent, happy,' said Gillian Hallett when Phoebe arrived for her usual afternoon counselling session. She sounded almost accusing, as if happiness were sinful. Her pale blue eyes looked moist and reproachful. Tears were not far away.

Phoebe felt that she ought to apologise or feel guilty but she knew that that was ridiculous. She wasn't exactly flaunting her happiness by being deliberately over-exuberant—she was just being her usual friendly self. She musn't let her patient's depression get to her, however much she empathised with her.

Gillian must accept that other people had a right to be happy. What would Josh advise? Phoebe guessed that he would tell her to be honest—he believed in being honest with the patients.

On one occasion he had said, 'We work on the softly, softly, approach most of the time but it is sometimes necessary to be blunt and not pull any punches. You can't always protect your patient or stop them being hurt. Sometimes it is not in their best interest to do so. There's no rule about it. Only instinct can tell you when and how to act.'

Gillian was sitting in her favourite spot at the table by the window. Phoebe sat down opposite her, reached across and took both her hands, cold as always in spite of the blazing sunshine, in her own. She chafed them gently and said softly, 'You're right. I am happy, though it's no big deal. I'm simply looking forward to having dinner with a friend tonight.'

Gillian's hands trembled. 'A man?'

'Yes.'

'Is he special?'

Phoebe hesitated. She hadn't expected such

a question. After a moment she said firmly, 'Yes, he is.'

'It's Dr Richmond, isn't it?'

Startled, Phoebe sucked in her breath. 'How did you know that?' she asked.

Gillian shrugged. 'Heard rumours. I've seen you both walking in the garden or going down the drive together. . .that's all, really. He's got a load of charisma and charm. Everyone seems to fall for him. It wouldn't be surprising if you did.' Her soft, pale blue eyes hardened. 'But don't be fooled by him. He may be a damned good doctor but he's just a man and they're all the same.' Her voice was incredibly harsh and bitter.

I'm not making any progress with her at all, thought Phoebe. Nothing touches her. I don't seem to be able to break through the barrier of her despair. She just hates herself, the world and, especially, men. And not so long ago I felt like that—when Neil and I parted. The trauma of rejection, Josh calls it, whether through death or desertion.

She squeezed Gillian's thin hands between her own. 'Not all men are all bad,' she said evenly.

'Wanna bet?' rasped Gillian crudely, pulling her hands free. Then, in a less abrasive tone, she murmured, 'Just don't get hurt, that's all.'

'Don't worry, I won't be,' Phoebe said firmly and, crossing her fingers behind her back, added to herself—not this time.

She was in the shower cubicle when there was a bang on the door and a muffled voice called, 'Phoebe, you're wanted on the phone. It's Doc Josh.'

Her heart plummeted as she bundled herself into a towelling robe and mules and padded along the hall to the telephone. Some instinct told her what she was going to hear.

She picked up the receiver. 'Hello,' she said in a detached little voice.

'Phoebe! You've guessed, haven't you?' His shadow sight even operated over the phone!

'Our date's off.'

'Yes. I'm so sorry, my dear, an emergency's cropped up. The hazards of being a doctor but you understand about that. It's the chap we admitted this morning, Alistair Gibbons. He's in a hell of a state. I've left him for a few minutes to phone you but I'll have to go back to him. He says he wants to talk. I hope he can—before he goes right over the edge.' He paused for a moment, then said quietly, 'Oh, Phoebe, one feels so bloody inadequate at times like this. I—I just hope I can help the poor guy.'

It was strange to hear the uncertainty in his voice. He was usually so confident. She wanted to reassure him. She'd read somewhere that even counsellors needed counselling: she wished that there was something wise and helpful she could say but all she could think of saying was, 'If anyone can, you can, Josh.'

'Do you mean that?' He sounded surprised. He was certainly not arrogant where his work was concerned.

'Of course. You've helped so many people. It's not just that you're a trained counsellor, you're solid and reassuring. Patients look on you as their friend as well as their doctor. You've got a great gift, Josh. Don't doubt it, for heaven's sake. Get out there and use it.' She was surprised by her own boldness but knew that it was the right thing to say. Right now he needed someone to restore his usual confidence.

He chuckled. 'Bolstering me up, Phoebe? You sound just like Granny. It's the sort of thing she would say if she was here.'

Like his grandmother? What a compliment! 'You will be pleased to see her back from her holiday.'

'I will, indeed. As you know, she's special to me—a wise, kind lady whom I love dearly.'

She could hear the affection in his voice. 'Yes, I felt that when I met her.'

'Pity she was off on holiday soon after you arrived. I hope you'll see a lot more of her when she returns and get to know each other better. You made a very favourable impression on her at your first meeting, you know.'

'Did I?' she murmured breathlessly, her pulses racing. So his grandmother liked her and he was pleased to tell her so.

That must mean that he *did* care for her. And if he did then surely he would understand about her reservations where men were concerned. What a pity that they were not meeting tonight, when she might have found the courage to confide in him and wipe out this morning's misunderstanding. Well, at least she could be honest with him now and let him know how much she regretted their broken date. She drew in a deep involuntary breath.

'I'm so *very* sorry that you can't make it tonight, Josh. I was looking forward immensely to our having dinner together, just the two of us.'

'You say that as if you really mean it.' He sounded almost surprised by the warmth in her voice.

'I do.'

He said softly, 'I know it sounds ridiculous but I'm glad you're disappointed. You didn't seem very keen on the idea this morning.'

'I said some silly things this morning.'

'And I didn't help. I lost my rag.' There was a moment's silence and then he said with a muttered expletive, 'Look, I've got to go but we'll fix another tête-à-tête soon.' And then, in an incredibly gentle tone, he murmured, 'Goodnight, love. Sleep well.'

'You too, Josh. Goodnight.' Carefully she replaced the receiver and slowly, her mind a maelstrom of emotions, made her way back to her room.

As it turned out there was no question of fixing a date over the next few days as there was an avalanche of admissions. A large batch of residents, mostly short-stay holiday people, went home and new residents were admitted in their places. But there were no holiday-makers among the new arrivals, who were all patients who had been discharged precipitately from Heresham Hospital while urgent building work was carried out. Some of the new admissions were barely convalescent.

Most of them were recovering from recent operations or acute medical conditions and needed skilled nursing care and for a short while the trained staff were under considerable pressure.

There were pulse and temperature and fluid charts to be filled in and painkilling or sedative injections and drugs to be given at intervals throughout the night as well as the day. Surgical dressings had to be changed and blood pressures to be taken. They were all procedures that had to be performed by registered nurses. Part of Richmond Place was for a while like a mini-hospital.

Everyone rallied round and Maeve, Phoebe and other members of the nursing team took it in turns to cover the nights to assist and supervise the auxiliary and care staff.

Phoebe was relieved to have her nights as

well as her days filled with work for it meant that her meetings with Josh took place when she was on duty and there was no opportunity for personal exchanges. And she found it easier to cope with her jumbled feelings on a professional rather than a personal basis.

She was aware that had their dinner date materialised as planned things might have been different for she had been in the mood to open up to him that night. She had felt so close to him when he had phoned. They had seemed, briefly, perfectly in accord. But the certainty that she had felt then that all would be well faded as the days passed and she succumbed once again to a flurry of doubts about their relationship.

Josh was frantically busy advising about the treatment of the new arrivals, as well as maintaining the medical and counselling care of the long-term residents, and gave no sign of his feelings for her. He was every inch the dedicated doctor—caring, warm and kind to the patients; unfailingly polite and friendly in a detached professional manner toward the staff, to whom he issued firm, brisk orders.

Phoebe's admiration for him grew over those

busy days and she didn't resent in the least his devotion to his patients or his coolness towards herself. And she was honest enough to admit that the heavy workload was a sound reason to put matters between them on hold for the time being. She worried, however, about how hard Josh was working and wished that he could have someone with whom to share the medical burden. But there wasn't anyone and she, like the rest of the staff, worked overtime to ease his load.

But, in spite of not minding that Josh was immersed in his work, as the blisteringly hot, sunny days and warm, sultry nights passed she found that seeing so much of him as they both put in long hours was a mixed blessing.

Whenever he appeared she was conscious of his mane of tawny blond hair glowing like a halo round his proud head, adding inches to his already impressive height. She was conscious, too, of the neat, silky stubble that framed his mobile mouth and strong, square jaw and strayed down the firm column of his throat. And the longing to run her fingers through his hair and stroke his beard was at times overwhelming.

The sight and the masculine scent of him

never failed to thrill her and send a frisson of delight and sheer undiluted pleasure coursing through her.

She even had to admit to herself that his beard suited him and was part and parcel of the whole man with whom she had fallen so completely in love.

Her love for him seemed to grow daily more intense. If they met and accidentally touched her skin tingled where it brushed against his and she would draw back as if burnt. And she wondered how long she would need to keep up this farce of being just good friends when she ached for so much more.

She had come near the other evening to revealing that she was in love with him and though he had been infinitely tender when he'd wished her goodnight she wondered how he would have reacted had she confessed that.

He had made it clear that he wanted to have a closer relationship with her but a permanent one based firmly on love and marriage—however much he might be attracted to her—was unlikely! Yet she wouldn't opt for anything less. This time it would be total commitment or nothing.

Probably he would run a mile, she thought sadly, if he knew where her thoughts were taking her. Love, combined with marriage, would frighten off most men and there was no reason to suppose that he would react any differently. A relationship, yes, but marriage?

Or was she wildly wrong about that? Was he halfway in love with her, drawn to her as helplessly as she was to him? Or did he see her as someone to fill the void left by his broken love affair which, though he dismissed as being firmly behind him, she sometimes doubted? Did part of him still hanker after his lost love? Was he looking for a substitute for the woman who had walked out of his life? And was she, Phoebe, that substitute? A second fiddle?

Yet he had seemed pleased that his beloved grandmother, old Lady Richmond, had liked her. Surely that had to be significant.

Could Maeve have been right when she had suggested that Josh had 'fancied her rotten' right from her first day at Richmond Place?

Could that be true? Was the sometimes remote man who had been jilted by the woman he loved capable of falling in love again? And if he was, was he ready to fall in love with her, Phoebe Palmer?

The question was niggling in the back of her mind and she was trying to will it away and concentrate on what she was doing when, on the second night she was on duty, Josh appeared in the dispensary where she was working.

She was balancing on a little stepladder sorting out the dressing packs, which were on the top shelf, when he spoke from the doorway.

'Hi,' he said softly in a low, slow drawl. 'All quiet on the hospital front?'

She jumped—she hadn't heard him coming. The hairs on the back of her neck curled and a shiver went up her spine at the sound of his voice. For once she hadn't been alerted to his nearby presence. The ladder wobbled and she wobbled with it. He crossed from the door in a couple of strides, put his hands round her waist and lifted her down effortlessly.

'Sorry about that. I didn't mean to give you a fright.' He was grinning, his eyes glinting like sapphires between his heavy lids.

Phoebe said breathlessly, indignantly, very conscious of the warmth of his hands round her waist, 'I might have fallen.'

'But you didn't. I saved you.' His rich, deep voice was velvet soft.

She tried to ignore the waves of nervous pleasure washing over her as he linked his hands behind her back and drew her closer. 'My white knight to the rescue,' she said, heavily sarcastic, making a rather feeble effort to ease herself away from him. And she added with a throaty laugh, 'I suppose you want a favour in return.'

Now why the hell did I say that? she asked herself as soon as the words were out of her mouth. I'm flirting with him. I want him to kiss me. I'm playing with fire. Her heartbeats galloped and her breast heaved.

'A kiss, just a friendly kiss, wouldn't come amiss,' he replied with a grin. 'A small favour from my lady, as the Bard might have said.'

Warning bells rang in her head. She musn't let herself go. She must get control of herself— of the situation. In spite of what he had said on the phone and the disappointment of their broken dinner date perhaps to him it was just a game between friends, maybe nothing more, but to her. . . She steeled herself not to tremble.

His closeness was making her feel almost faint. She had never seen him quite like this before. He was almost boyish, neither the mature, solid man who had comforted her under the portico in the storm nor the sophisticated, sexy man of the world who had embraced her so fiercely on the bridge.

He was in a strange, ebullient, teasing, almost *loving* mood! She thought her heart would stop. Was that possible? His eyes were bright and gleaming, intense as they swept over her face, seeming to drink in every detail as if searching for something.

The house was quiet. The care assistants were working upstairs and the patients, for the moment, sleeping peacefully. The witching hour of midnight, she thought fancifully, though in fact it was nearly two o'clock.

She swallowed and said in what she hoped was a cool, rather reproving voice, praying that he wouldn't see how defenceless she was beneath the veneer, 'You should be so lucky. This lady doesn't give her favours away that easily and certainly not when she's on duty.'

'Not even to her boss?'

'Especially not to her boss.'

'Oh, my dear, that's a pity,' he said huskily.

His eyes caught and held hers and she stared into them, mesmerised.

She tried to pull away from his hands, which were still locked round her, but couldn't and neither could she drag her eyes away from his. It was just as it had been before when she had drowned in their fabulous blue depths. She was vaguely aware of the gleaming white and chrome of the dispensary with its shelves packed with bottles of tablets and liquids as he held her close and his eyes burned into hers.

Spellbound, she almost stopped breathing as wave after wave of delight washed over her and the world around them dissolved into nothingness and she knew that her eyes said what her lips could not. . .I love you.

And *his* eyes were speaking volumes too. They were full of passion, full of longing, embracing her, enfolding her. . .

The low-key night buzzer hummed and a light flashed on the nurse call display board over the door.

Phoebe jerked back to the present and blinked. 'Oh,' she murmured as she exhaled a long, pent-up breath. 'I must go. A patient. . .I'm so sorry.'

All passion fled from Josh's eyes. A veil came down. 'Are you, Phoebe?' he said bitterly. 'Is it genuinely a case of duty calls, even if there are other people around to take care of things? Or could it be an easy way out—yet another way of saying hands off? How very sad. I thought that since our telephone conversation the other night things might be different between us.'

Phoebe felt the colour mount in her cheeks. 'I don't know what you mean,' she whispered.

But she did know. He hadn't liked it because she had ended their kiss. His male ego had been hurt. He had let his mask slip, had revealed some deep emotion when he had stared into her eyes and had let her see that he cared, and now he felt rejected.

He unlocked his hands from round her waist and placed them on her shoulders, giving them a gentle squeeze. 'Don't you, Phoebe? I thought you were beginning to understand me,' he said softly, and dropped a kiss on the tip of her nose. 'I thought I was beginning to get through to you but it seems that I was wrong. I'll have to be patient a little longer,' and, with a dismissive shrug, he turned his head and flicked a look at the display board and said abruptly, 'Eighteen—that's Mrs Howard's room isn't it?' He dropped his hands from her shoulders and took a step backwards.

What did he mean, he'd have to be patient a little longer? Patient about what? It didn't make sense. And this sudden change of manner from the intimate to the impersonal was chilling, frightening. She looked at his impassive face as he waited for her answer. There was no help there. He had said all he was going to say, for the moment at least.

Her heart in her mouth, Phoebe nodded and with a tremendous effort gathered herself together. 'Yes,' she said, striving to sound coolly professional to match his coolness. 'She's the post-op cholecystectomy patient whom you saw you saw on admission earlier today.

'She's quite poorly tonight and still vomiting occasionally. I was going to ask you to have a look at her. She's on Maxolon T.D.S. but I think she may need something else. I don't think that Maxolon three times a day is enough. She's getting a lot of abdominal pain and her surgical wound's rather messy. We're having to change the dressing pretty frequently to keep it clean.

'Right now she's probably buzzing because she wants help to go to the loo. We've told her that she musn't attempt to get out of bed without assistance at present.'

'Quite right. I wrote her up for a sedative when I saw her on admission. She's had that, of course?'

'Yes, at ten, so she's had a few hours' sleep.'

'Poor old thing. She's had a rough time, with the op not being as straightforward as it might have been and the bile duct as well as the gall bladder being inflamed.' He rubbed his hand over his bearded jaw and looked thoughtful.

'I'm surprised that they didn't incise the duct or put in a separate drain when they operated. It was the obvious thing to do and would have made the poor old thing more comfortable.' He frowned at Phoebe almost as if it was her fault that the surgeon had failed to do the obvious. Then he said tersely, 'OK. Let's go and see our Mrs Howard and do what we can for her.' And, turning on his heel, he strode toward the door.

Phoebe stared at his retreating back. What to make of him? Damn him and his shadow sight. She wished she had some of it and could get a clue as to what made him tick. A wave of anger swept over her. He seemed to have dismissed all that had passed between them minutes before. So his ego was hurt because she hadn't understood him and hadn't responded to him immediately! Well, her ego was hurt too. Why hadn't he *told* her how he felt and not made enigmatic remarks about her not understanding?

What *was* she supposed to understand from the long, eloquent look that they had exchanged? Had he been saying that he loved her? Or had he discovered that she loved him and expected her to fall into his arms like a ripe plum? Yes, that was it. She had completely given herself away when she'd kissed him, unable to conceal her love. Her cheeks burned at the thought.

But he had been in a curious, flirty sort of mood from the moment he'd arrived in the dispensary, so unlike his usual self. It was as if he was battening down his emotions, suppressing something. Well, whatever it was, the buzzer had put a stop to that.

The buzzer! He was quite right. She had used it to break off their embrace. It hadn't been an emergency buzzer. She had known that the care assistants would answer the call. She *had* simply used it as an excuse to put an end to something that she couldn't control. No wonder he was angry.

Those few minutes in his arms had been magic. Tonight had changed everything between them. They could never carry on as if nothing had happened.

Her mind seething, she followed him along the corridor, through the dimly lit reception hall and up the stairs. With his long legs and in spite of his limp he took these two at a time. His back was rigid. He seemed almost a stranger, aloof and unreachable.

At the top of the stairs he paused and leaned on the balcony rail as he waited for her to catch up with him. 'Come here,' he said low-voiced but commanding as she hesitated on the top step. 'There's no hurry for Mrs Howard. We'll put in an appearance when the care staff have done their stuff.'

Tense and unsure of herself and not knowing what to expect of him, Phoebe moved over to stand beside him. But it seemed that he was no longer angry. He immediately slipped an arm round her shoulders and gave her a reassuring squeeze. At the unexpectedly tender touch she tensed even more. 'Relax,' he murmured. 'Trust me, all is going to be well. You just need time.'

She shivered and felt icy cold inside. Trust him! It might have been Neil speaking. That was his line after they had quarrelled, telling her to trust him. God, what a joke that was. She said in a hard little voice, 'Why should I trust you? Why should I trust any man?'

There was a moment's silence and then he said in a matter-of-fact tone, not looking at her but staring into the half-darkness, 'Because I'm not any man. I'm the man who happens to be in love with you.'

In the half-light of the balcony Phoebe gaped at his handsome profile for endless moments in stunned silence. From the shadow-shrouded reception hall below came the steady rhythmic tick of the grandfather clock.

'In love!' she whispered at last. 'In love?'

Josh dropped his arm from her shoulders and turned to look at her. 'Yes,' he said flatly. 'In love. It's what you wanted to hear, isn't it?'

Her heart hammered crazily. He had read her as always like a book. It was unbelievable. He couldn't mean it. She wanted to believe it but couldn't believe it. He was just saying that to placate her. 'But—but you can't be. You're still in love with. . .'

'With whom, Phoebe?' His voice was suddenly cool, his face expressionless.

'With—with your ex-fiancée,' she mumbled through dry lips, recoiling from his coldness.

He shook his head slowly from side to side. 'Oh, Phoebe, what am I going to do with you? I thought that, given a little time. . .' He shrugged and cupped her chin in one large hand and she trembled like a leaf. 'Can't you see that you're using that as an excuse? You're afraid to commit yourself.'

'No, that's not true,' she denied, stepping back from him, anger lending strength to her shaky voice.

'Oh, but it is, my dear. You're in one hell of an emotional mess and we've got to sort it out so that you can accept my love, which you're hell-bent on rejecting. We've got to talk, though obviously now's not the time or place. Come down to my cottage this evening. I'll feed you and we'll sort things out.'

It was a cold, flat command, not an invitation. How dared he? 'I can't,' she said quickly. 'I've made other arrangements.' Who was he to dictate to her?

'*If* you've made other arrangements, break them,' he said harshly.

'People will think all sorts of things if they see me going to your cottage.'

'Then, for God's sake, let them,' he ground out in a low voice. 'What the hell does it matter? We're grown-up people. We can do our own thing. You need to get yourself straightened out. I want to know if it's just me or men in general who are giving you problems and I want the truth, with no prevaricating. You must open up and come clean with me. Let me into your past—don't shut me out. I'll expect you at the cottage at seven. Be there, Phoebe.' The words came out savagely in short staccato sentences.

Her senses reeled. How could a man who had just said that he was in love with her be so brisk, business-like and angry? Maybe he was right about her being afraid to commit herself but she wasn't going to be the only one to come clean. He had some explaining to do too.

Well, she wouldn't be ordered about. Neil used to boss her about. She had been like putty in his hands but no man was going to get to her like that ever again, not even Josh—much as she loved him. It would be so easy to throw herself into his arms and let him take charge of her life—allow him to straighten her out. After all, that was his job—straightening people out. But that wouldn't do. They would meet on equal terms or not at all.

Josh's voice broke into her racing, mixed-up thoughts. He said sharply, 'Phoebe, say something.'

Anger gave her courage. She lifted her chin and stared at him across the small space that separated them and said in a clear, firm, voice, 'Yes, I'll be at the cottage tonight and we'll talk. But we have to be honest with each other, Josh. It must be a fair exchange. I won't let you steamroller me. I need to know things about you too.'

He was silent for a moment as he stared back at her, face and eyes expressionless. Then he said levelly, 'OK, a quid pro quo it is,' and added enigmatically, 'You're a brave girl and I love you.' Phoebe's heart lurched at the words. He smiled slightly.

'And now back to work. Let's go and see what we can do for Mrs Howard,' and turning on his heel he strode across the balcony and disappeared through the elegantly curved archway leading to the residents' rooms.

For the second time that evening Phoebe stared blankly at his retreating back. She didn't know how he could appear so detached and carry on as if nothing had happened after saying that he loved her but if he could do it, so could she. As always, personal and professional pride came to her aid. She had a job to do, she thought grimly, and she would damn well do it. Smothering her feelings, she sped after him down the long corridor.

Two of the night-care assistants were with Mrs Howard when Josh and Phoebe arrived in her room. She was lying back against a mound of pillows looking pale and drawn, her eyes closed and her face screwed up with pain.

Josh smiled a greeting to the carers, then crossed the room and stood looking down at the frail lady in the bed.

'She's just been sick,' whispered one of the helpers to Phoebe. 'Projectile vomiting. Went everywhere.' She was holding a covered receiver in her hand, while the other helper was bundling up sheets and pillow cases. 'We've cleaned her up and changed everything and given her a sip of water. Is there anything else we can do?'

'No, thanks,' replied Phoebe. 'We'll sort out Mrs Howard.' She gestured toward the bundle of dirty linen. 'You'd better deal with that lot and see that all is well downstairs. Doctor will do a round of the other poorly ones when we've finished here.'

They spent twenty minutes with Mrs Howard. Phoebe renewed the dressing to her surgical wound, which was oozing a slightly bloody exudate, and when she had finished Josh examined his patient's abdomen with long, gentle fingers and talked to her reassuringly.

'We can do quite a lot to help the sickness,' he explained. 'It's partly caused through your operation, to which you haven't adjusted yet, and partly through your hiatus hernia, which causes a reflux action in your oesophagus. This is what's causing you pain. When you try to swallow food or even your saliva it gets pushed back up your gullet and into your mouth, making you sick. But don't worry; we'll soon have you feeling more comfortable.

'I'm going to sort out some new medication

for you, an immediate injection which will help slow down this action and another to reduce the nausea. We'll also start you off on Gaviscon, a soothing liquid which will alleviate some of the pain and discomfort in your stomach.'

Gently he patted one of the pale, parchment-like hands that lay on the coverlet. 'Now, Mrs Howard, Staff Nurse is going to make you comfortable and you're going to sleep well for the rest of the night. That's doctor's orders.' He smiled down at her and then across the bed at Phoebe and she found herself smiling back as a warm glow spread through her. 'I'd like a word,' he said, moving swiftly toward the door.

'I'll be back in a few minutes,' Phoebe assured Mrs Howard, stopping to squeeze her hand and smooth the top sheet before following Josh from the room.

He was leaning against the wall beside the door, scribbling on the patient's treatment chart. Surreptitiously she studied his serious, absorbed face as he concentrated on what he was writing. And when a moment later he looked up from the chart she knew by the humorous, and at the same time tender, gleam in his eyes that he had been conscious of her watching him and, to her annoyance, she blushed furiously. So much for being cool and professional.

'Very nice,' he said softly. 'I'm glad you can still blush, Phoebe. So few women do these days.'

Phoebe swallowed and said through tight lips, 'I wish to God I didn't. It's just a reflex action; it doesn't mean anything.'

Josh grinned broadly. 'Of course it doesn't,' he agreed soothingly and not giving her time to retort, thrust the treatment chart towards her and, resuming his professional mode, said briskly, 'I've written Mrs Howard up for an injection of Stemetil 2 ml to be given immediately and again at ten a.m. if required. That should take care of her nausea.

'I also want her to have Cimetidine 200 mg intramuscularly four-hourly over the next twelve hours and then orally in tablet form. And start her off any time on the Gaviscon.

'And I'm sure I don't have to remind you to press fluids to restore the fluids lost through the vomiting.'

Phoebe bristled as she took the chart from him. 'No,' she said fiercely, matching his briskness, 'You don't have to remind me of that: it's basic routine for any well-trained nurse.' Her eyes flashed and her lips compressed in a straight line.

Josh gave a subdued snort of laughter and bent forward and kissed her firmly on her angry mouth. 'Oh, Phoebe, you're priceless. So dedicated—all that a nurse should be.' He stopped laughing and, suddenly serious, murmured, 'And all that a woman should be, too, and I love you.' Then, pushing himself away from the wall, he strode away down the long corridor.

She didn't see him again that night as by the time she had finished attending to Mrs Howard he had completed his round and left the building.

Feeling remote and detached from reality with the memory of that swift kiss lingering on her lips, she somehow got through the rest of her duty period with her usual calm efficiency. She refused to allow herself to think about Josh and his earlier anger and what he had said about loving her. Only when she went off duty at eight, after handing over to Maeve, did she let herself dwell on what he had said.

His final words—'I love you'—buzzed like

a fly in the back of her head. She picked distractedly at her food, discovering that she wasn't really hungry as she breakfasted with the other staff who had been on night duty and made herself join in their inconsequential chatter.

Not until she'd escaped to her room and undressed and showered, set the alarm and eventually crawled thankfully under the duvet had she allowed them to take over completely.

She hugged herself with a kind of tremulous, uncertain joy as she lay in bed, mulling over those magic words. 'I love you', that he had uttered in the wee small hours of the morning, the witching hours. Had he really said that? Yes! Had he meant it? He must have done. He'd said it twice, once on the balcony and once in the corridor, and on neither occasion had he sounded sloshy or sentimental, just cool and factual.

Too factual, too cool? She sat bolt upright, clasping her hands about her knees. Could he say that he was in love with her and be so calm about it, so unemotional? What had he said on the balcony? 'It's what you wanted to hear!'

So had he simply been trying to please her when he'd uttered them? Was he after all only seeking a replacement for the woman who had left him high and dry and, sensing that Phoebe wouldn't readily step into that role on a casual basis, had used the magic word—*love*—to entice her into a relationship with him?

'*No*!' she muttered fiercely to the empty room. 'He wouldn't do that.' But he might if he thought that it would make you happy, said a treacherous little voice in her head. If he realises that you are in love with him it's just the sort of generous thing he might do.

She stared unseeingly into space for endless minutes until, suddenly overwhelmed by tiredness, she fell back on her pillow and drifted off into a troubled, dream-haunted sleep in which both Josh and Neil appeared.

Their images were distorted, wraith-like, their bearded faces ferociously angry as they charged towards each other through a mist against a backdrop of icy mountains. And they were uttering blood-curdling yells and waving swords which met and crashed together as she woke with a start, sweating and shivering.

The alarm which she had set for three o'clock in the afternoon was shrilling insistently.

CHAPTER NINE

JOSH! His image floated before Phoebe's closed lids as she surfaced into wakefulness—the thick, tawny blond hair, the strong jaw-line beneath the close cropped beard, the intensely blue eyes, the aristocratic aquiline nose.

Her stomach churned, alive with butterflies. . . The man she loved; the man who, in the middle of the night, had suddenly announced that he loved her; the man she didn't, couldn't, quite believe! But why couldn't she?

She recalled the unhappy thoughts that had overwhelmed her just before she had fallen into an exhausted sleep. The doubts that had chased through her mind as she remembered not only *what* he had said as they had stood side by side on the balcony but *how* he had said it in a flat, almost disinterested voice. It was hard to believe in such a cold, matter-of-fact statement of love.

But she wanted to believe him. He wasn't really a cold man but a warm, sexy, virile man. His coldness and his remoteness were only skin-deep, a façade that he sometimes wore. She remembered her dream sharply and clearly— Josh and Neil fighting, fighting to the death— fighting over her. There had been nothing cold and matter-of-fact about that. Of course it was only a dream but a vivid dream and his sharp image was still there.

Cautiously she opened her eyes. The image disappeared and she lifted her head from the pillow and looked round the familiar room, glowing rosily in the curtain-dimmed sunlight that filled the window. She stretched out a hand and switched off the alarm, remembering as she did so why she had set it for three o'clock. She planned to visit Gillian Hallett.

Of course she needn't go, didn't have to, not after being on night duty and especially after what had happened last night between her and Josh. She should be trying to resolve her own problems, not meddling in someone else's. But she had promised Gillian and habit died hard. If you made a promise to a patient you jolly well kept it.

Anyway, she couldn't think straight so she might as well push her own muddled, unhappy thoughts into the background in order to pay her regular afternoon visit to her special patient. She hadn't missed a day yet in spite of the pressure of work caused by the new intake of ill residents and no way was she going to miss out today on account of her personal mixed-up feelings.

Hopefully the effort would be worth it. The daily visits were just beginning to pay off. Gillian had allowed her to wash and blow-dry her hair one afternoon. And she had begun to open up a little in a brittle fashion, talking about herself and her husband, Larry, and the marriage that had obviously begun to crumble long before she had had her mastectomy.

Of her own volition, though perhaps unconsciously, she was beginning to peel away layer after layer of hurt and anger and bitterness that had built up over the years but had remained hidden until exposed by the trauma of her operation.

To Phoebe Larry was being revealed as a chauvinistic, selfish and uncaring man, not the noble, patient, long-suffering husband that Gillian had initially portrayed. It was quite clear that she, and not he, had done all the giving. And yet she still seemed to be convinced that she, and not he, had caused their marriage to break down.

Would she ever stop blaming herself for what had happened or would the truth begin to dawn on her as she unmasked her feelings? And if it did would it help her to come to terms with her condition and her future, deprived of her husband, and made ugly——as she saw it——by the loss of her breast?

For nothing would convince her that, when dressed, her near-perfect prosthesis looked quite normal and nobody would guess that she had had a mastectomy.

'It might *look* that way,' she'd said stonily when Phoebe, using that argument, had suggested that they go for a walk in the garden, 'but *I* know that it isn't for real and I look a freak. I *am* a freak.' And nothing that Phoebe could say would convince her otherwise and she had spent the rest of the afternoon trying to break through the icy barrier that her distraught patient had once more erected.

Reporting to Josh as she updated him on the progress she was making with Gillian, Phoebe had asked, 'Even if she does talk her way through her problems will it make her happier to know that her operation or the fact that they didn't have children wasn't responsible for the break up of her marriage? Or perhaps is only partially responsible and that Larry would probably have left her for another woman anyway? It's strange—she hates him and all men, yet doesn't blame him for leaving her.'

'I simply have no idea whether it will help,' replied Josh gravely, his eyes sombre as he raked long fingers through his hair in a now-familiar gesture. 'I wish to God I had. It's not like putting on a tourniquet and stopping a haemorrhage where one can see that the treatment's effective.

'In spite of advances in psychological medicine we don't yet know much about the control of deep-seated emotional trauma, though it's pretty obvious that it helps to root out its real cause and talking often does this. But that in itself may be painful which is why it *must* be a voluntary process and the outcome isn't predictable.'

'So you can never tell if it's going to work?

'No. That's why we don't offer advice but a listening service. The answers come from the patients themselves. But it's amazing how often they do talk their way through devastating experiences and find their own solutions. Sometimes it comes after weeks or months of self-questioning. Sometimes a happening, an incident, can trigger it off and sometimes,' he said sadly, 'it doesn't happen at all.'

'But supposing Gillian asks me a direct question—asks for advice—should I give it?'

'Depends what the question is. You can venture an opinion if you feel sure of yourself—a qualified opinion as a friend which might help her sort out her muddled thoughts and make sense of them. But that may be the most you can do, Phoebe.' He touched her cheek with gentle fingers and said softly, 'Be wise but don't play God.'

'I wouldn't *dream* of it,' she'd replied indignantly.

'No, of course you wouldn't, not intentionally. You're too good a nurse. But, believe me, it's easy to be tempted. Somebody else's problems may seem to you to be simple and you might feel that you have the answer. But emotional problems are never simple. I repeat, the most you can do to help your patient is to offer to accompany her through the maze of her emotions.'

And with that piece of advice she had had to be content for at that moment the phone rang and she had left him to answer it.

And now, her mind buzzing with thoughts of Josh and the meeting she was to have with him that evening, she recalled this conversation of a few days earlier as she struggled out of bed and got ready to visit Gillian.

'That's what I could do with,' she muttered, savagely towelling herself dry following a cold, invigorating shower, 'someone to walk with me through the maze and help me unravel the ideas in *my* muddled head.'

Someone wise and clever like Josh would do nicely if he weren't the main part of the muddle, she thought wryly. She slipped into a minuscule strapless bra and pants and a long, loose, cotton dress, printed in a leafy mosaic of pale greens and browns and soft yellows on a creamy background.

The muted colours and the pattern they made as they merged with each other seemed to match her mood of damped-down, jumbled emotions, she thought, as she made her way down to

Gillian's room a little later. She wouldn't change—she would wear it tonight when she visited Josh at his cottage. It would be most appropriate—a dress to compliment her uncertain state of mind.

'Please, God,' she whispered to herself as she walked along the corridor, 'let everything come out right tonight. Let's be honest with each other. Let him *really* be in love with me and not just pretending for an altruistic or any other reason.'

Gillian was standing by the window, staring down at the sunlit garden, when Phoebe knocked and entered her room.

She didn't look round but said in a quavery, despairing, incredulous voice, 'How can they do it? How can they bear to do it? They don't seem to mind about people looking at them. There's a man down there without proper arms—just stumps with metal things fitted to them—and he's laughing as if it didn't matter.

'And the girl with him is dreadfully deformed. She's walking with crutches and she's laughing, too, and she's got such a pretty face and they're so brave and I. . . I. . .' Her voice rose shrilly and then trailed off and she turned an anguished face to Phoebe, tears streaming down her cheeks.

Phoebe sped across the room and put her arms round her. 'That's right, Gillian, love, have a good cry,' she murmured. 'It'll do you good; don't bottle it up any longer.'

For a long time Phoebe stood with her arms wrapped round Gillian's thin, shuddering body as she sobbed noisily like a child. Is this it? she wondered as she crooned words of comfort and stroked the pale blonde hair. Is this the real breakthrough? Is this what Josh had meant when he'd said that people often talked their way through their problems?

Or had this sudden collapse been triggered off by a specific event? Had the obvious cheerfulness and courage of the armless young man and his companion succeeded in shattering the icy barriers which Gillian hid behind?

It was as if a dam had burst as the tears that had been held back for so long were released. But would that free her? Would she be able to rebuild her life?

When the tears eventually came to a hiccuping stop Gillian said shakily, with a glimmer of a smile, 'I think I'm all cried out. Thanks.'

She blew her nose and slipped out of Phoebe's arms and slumped down in a chair by the table, dropping her head in her hands. 'Hell, I'm tired. I could sleep for a week,' she muttered wearily. 'I haven't cried like that since I was a little girl.'

Phoebe said softly, 'You need to rest. Come and lie down.' She moved over to the bed and turned down the coverlet and duvet.

'Brilliant idea,' said Gillian in an exhausted voice and walked with slow, dragging steps across the room and collapsed on the bed. 'Stay with me,' she muttered, stretching out a hand as Phoebe pulled the covers over her, 'until I go to sleep.'

She fell asleep in an instant but her eyelids trembled and her breathing was shallow and uneven and Phoebe sat beside her for a long time, stroking the thin, cold hand that lay in hers and waiting until her breathing became deep and regular. Only then did she release Gillian's hand and steal softly from the room.

It was just after five-thirty. She had an hour or so to kill before going down to the cottage for her rendezvous with Josh. She didn't want to be alone. She was sick to death of her own befuddled thoughts which she couldn't unravel. She wanted company and presently found herself drifting along the softly scented, rose-covered pergola towards the swimming pool, which was bound to be cheerful and busy at this time of day.

The pool-house was pleasantly warm under its specially tinted plastic dome. She sat down on one of the coloured paving slabs edging the pool, removed her sandals and dabbled her feet in the sparkling water. Bliss!

The dome was pretty full but Maeve's brilliant red hair was unmissable as she bobbed about helping one of the physios and a care assistant exercise a paraplegic patient. She spotted Phoebe, waved and, after a few minutes, swam over and joined her.

'I'm off at six,' she said. 'Fancy a night out on the town? The film club in Heresham is showing that old weepy, *Brief Encounter*. We could have a meal and go on there afterwards.'

'Sorry, can't—not tonight. I've got something else on.'

Maeve arched her eyebrows and grinned. 'Oh, something important like your own brief encounter with the boss perhaps?' she said slyly, her green eyes sparkling.

How the devil did she know that? Concealing her surprise, Phoebe laughed with pretended nonchalance. 'Really, it's no big deal but, as a matter of fact, yes. How did you guess?'

Maeve's grin widened. 'Well I'm a good guesser and the grapevine has it that our Dr Josh spent a hell of a long time on his round in the early hours of this morning and not all of it with his patients.'

Phoebe groaned. 'I don't believe it. I'll murder those girls,' she grumbled. 'Half the time we were *talking* about the patients, even if we weren't with them.'

'And the other half?' asked Maeve with a chuckle, sliding back down into the water.

Fleetingly Phoebe wondered what Maeve's reaction would be if she told her of the bombshell that Josh had dropped by announcing that he loved her and of her own hesitant response to this.

She looked down at Maeve's bright, animated, kind, knowing face and thought that she probably wouldn't be surprised at all. In fact, with her Celtic insight, I bet she already knows what a confused state I'm in, Phoebe thought with a mixture of exasperation and resignation.

On cue, having peered into her mind, Maeve reached up and patted her knee with a wet hand. 'It's going to be all right, Phoeb, believe me,' she said, using the diminutive for her name that was a left-over of their training days. 'Everything's going to come good for you and Josh. I know it *here*.'

She thumped her chest over the region of her heart; and, not waiting for a response to this astonishing remark, shot off to the other side of the pool, leaving Phoebe staring after her totally bemused by her extraordinary perception.

It was a little after half-past six when she made her way slowly across the park to Josh's cottage, which was on the very edge of the estate in a small copse.

Maeve's words were still ringing in her ears, going round and round in her head. How come, she asked herself, that she's so sure that all will be well and has no doubts about how things are going to turn out? It's uncanny the way she sussed out how mixed up I am and tried to reassure me.

'So why the hell can't I be sure too?' she cried out angrily, punching the empty, still air above her head.

It was a warm, humid evening and muted hazy sunshine filtered out of a sky that had been a brilliant, translucent blue an hour before but which was now a sullen brassy canopy draped low over the treetops. It was a breathless, ominously quiet evening. No birds sang. That there was one hell of a storm brewing was obvious. She should have driven down to the cottage.

She shrugged, not really caring. With luck the rain would hold off for a bit and Josh would give her a lift back if it was raining later.

Choosing to walk had seemed like a good idea. It would force her to confront her see-sawing emotions. But however hard she tried she couldn't think straight; couldn't get command of her thoughts. They rambled all over the place.

Why on earth was she dreading, rather than looking forward to, this meeting with the man who only hours before had told her what she had longed to hear? Was it because he might tell her something that she'd rather not hear—perhaps inadvertently reveal that he still hankered for his ex-lover in spite of his denials to the contrary? Why, why, why couldn't she take them at face value?

Was it because she'd learned via the grapevine that his ex-fiancée had been beautiful, jet-setting and rich and she couldn't believe that he'd allowed himself to fall in love with a hard-working, passably attractive nurse?

Yes, that was part of it but, however unlikely it seemed, he *had* said quite firmly that he loved her so why couldn't she accept that? Surely not even to please her would he have pretended to love her. She should be on top of the world, not feeling as though she were walking on a knife-edge.

The smooth, cropped grass of the parkland gave way to rough pasture and she found herself walking through the tall grass of a meadow bordering the trees that shielded Josh's cottage. The meadow was dotted with bright blue cornflowers, snow-white marguerites and glistening yellow buttercups.

She must be nearly there. In a few minutes she would be with him in the privacy of his home and they would be alone together, just the two of them.

It occurred to her that they had never properly been alone before but always within sight or sound of patients or staff. She caught her breath and for a moment her sombre thoughts were overlaid by a thrill of pleasurable anticipation at the thought of being on her own with him. Perhaps all would be well after all and this awful feeling of foreboding that had been with her all day would disappear when she saw him.

She longed to believe in him; ached for his love. She was almost frightened of the intensity of her emotions—the sexual need of him and the spiritual need of him to make her whole and complete. She had felt this way ever since he had kissed her on the bridge with such sex-starved hunger on the evening she'd discovered that she loved him. A hunger which she had shared but had shied away from because she had wanted more than sex.

Well, now, if he was to be believed he *was* offering more than that. He was offering love.

She came to a halt in the middle of the meadow and clenched her fists until the knuckles shone whitely. Her head drooped and she stared down at the long grass and the flowers powdering her skirt with pollen. 'Please,

please,' she prayed in a fierce whisper, 'let him love me, really love me.'

A snowy-faced marguerite stared up at her and some quirky instinct made her bend and pick the heavy-headed blossom and begin systematically pulling off the petals, chanting rhythmically, 'He loves me, he loves me not.'

The repetitive jingle was soothing, momentarily dulling her senses. In the brassy yellow sunshine of a storm-laden summer's evening it was difficult to believe in the extraordinary conversation that had taken place in the dark early hours of morning between herself and Josh. And yet it had happened and her presence here proved it.

She pulled off the last petal as she reached the trees edging the wood. 'He loves me,' she murmured, and then suppressed a self-conscious giggle, feeling ridiculous, knowing that she was deliberately trivialising the situation and trying to escape from reality by playing with fate. As if a few tortured petals could influence the truth or the future!

What utter superstitious nonsense. With a contemptuous, jerky movement she threw away the mutilated flower-head; she was ashamed of herself for pretending, for playing a childish game. She had to face Josh and learn the truth from him. If he repeated that he loved her she would accept his word, not question it. She *must*, she *would* trust him.

Quite suddenly, out of the blue, a wave of hope surged through her and she *knew* with absolute certainty that all *was* going to be well, as Maeve had promised. The ice that had sat round her heart all day melted and the turmoil and doubt disappeared She and Josh would talk their way through their problems, just as they helped other people talk their way through theirs. And they would resolve them and be at one with each other.

At one, the two of them—never to be lonely again. Needing each other. Passionate friends, passionate lovers. It sounded wonderful. Was it possible? *Yes*, she wanted to shout. I love him and that's all that matters. All she needed now was the courage to tell him so.

With her heart thumping like a piston engine, she plunged into the dark mass beneath the trees and followed the short path through the wood that emerged almost opposite Josh's cottage.

The cottage was a thatched-roof, tile-hung,

long, low building surrounded by a lavender hedge and a garden full of old-fashioned flowers—delphiniums, larkspur and lupins, with masses of creamy yellow roses rambling over and round the porch. And to complete the picture of rural perfection a red brick path and a white wicket-gate.

It was idyllic—a perfect trysting place for lovers, Phoebe thought, a faint smile curving her lips at the fanciful idea. . . Lovers! Is that what she and Josh would be by the end of the evening?

Her pulses raced and a shiver ran up and down her spine as she savoured the thought of being in close, intimate, physical contact with him, of feeling his sensitive, clever hands exploring her naked body; and of her own hands stroking his muscle-hard belly and the golden curly hair on his broad chest.

She drew in a long, deep breath. . .and it was at that moment that Josh appeared.

He came swinging round the corner of the house balancing a long hoe on a broad shoulder, large and confident and looking so like the bold warrior Viking of her dream that she drew back into the shadows of the trees with a small startled gasp.

He must have heard or seen a movement for he looked across at the wood and called softly, a question in his voice, 'Phoebe?'

Feeling foolish and trying hard to appear non-chalant, she stepped out into the lane. 'Hi,' she said casually. 'It's such a lovely evening I thought I'd walk.'

Thunder rumbled round the horizon. Josh glanced up at the lowering yellow-ochre sky. 'Oh, yes, a lovely evening,' he teased with a wry grin and a caustically raised eyebrow as he strode down the path and opened wide the neat white gate. 'It isn't raining yet but, knowing your affinity for stormy weather, no doubt it will soon do so.'

His grin faded as she crossed the lane and reached the gate and he held out his hand and said quietly, 'Come in, my dear girl, welcome to my bolt-hole, my retreat.'

For a moment the deep, undisguised warmth of his welcome surprised her and she hesitated before slipping her hand, willing it not to tremble, into his. He grasped it firmly and drew her into the garden.

'Thank you,' she murmured, not knowing quite what she was thanking him for but not knowing what else to say.

Carefully Josh dropped his hoe onto the grass and took her other hand and, holding her at arm's length, said with quiet emphasis, 'Thank *you* for coming, Phoebe. My invitation last night was hardly what you might call gracious—in fact it was bloody rude. I wouldn't have blamed you for ignoring it.'

She shook her head. 'I couldn't do that. But why were you so cold, so angry, so high-handed, as if you were forced to say what you did but didn't really want to?'

'Shock tactics. Anything to break through to the real you, make you see that you love me and let you know who was boss. You had been responding to me when that bloody buzzer sounded—we were on the same wavelength but you used that as an excuse to back off. And then you said your piece about not trusting any man and that made me spitting mad, lumping me in with all men because you'd been hurt in the past.

'I needed to *make* you see sense and see that I was not just any man but the right man for you, the only man for you. I'd had enough of pussyfooting around.' The nostrils of his aquiline nose flared at the memory.

God, he was arrogant—so sure of himself. She forgot all her good intentions about believing him if he said that he loved her. Anger spurted through her. He'd no right to be so sure about her.

She stared steadily into his brilliant blue eyes. 'And what makes you think that I love you?' she asked in a tight voice.

With a monumental calm that made her itch to beat her fists on his broad chest he surveyed her angry face in silence and then said, levelly, 'Because I love you and am privy to your thoughts and feelings. Because we've been attracted to each other from the start. There's some sort of chemistry between us—you can't deny that.'

His eyes widened and softened. He still held her at arm's length but his hands tightened round her fingers and his thumbs stroked the back of her knuckles, making her inwardly tremble and long to throw herself into his arms.

To her dismay her anger started to ooze away and she struggled to hold onto it a little longer, to use it as a shield against the sheer masculine power of the man that threatened to swamp her. She had questions to ask and she wanted answers.

'No, I don't deny that,' she said snappishly, 'but chemistry's one thing and love's another. You said nothing about love that evening on the bridge. You talked about friendship, made a big deal of it. Why should I believe that you love me now?'

The corners of his mouth curved into a faint smile. He said in a soothing voice, as if comforting a fractious child, 'Because, my dear, dear Phoebe, you weren't ready for such a declaration then. You were afraid. You were in no mood to accept that I might be in love with you *and* want sex; want more than a one-night stand.

'Because of whatever had happened in your past the two seemed incompatible to you. You couldn't come to terms with that so you took the easy way out and accused me of still hankering after my ex-fiancée so that you didn't have to face your own sexual hang-ups.'

Anger surged back. 'Don't be so damned patronising,' she spat out. 'And what makes you think. . .?' She broke off as the sound of a car moving fast up the lane shattered the silence of the breathless, heavy, pre-storm evening air.

Josh pressed her fingers hard, his eyebrows coming together in a ferocious frown. 'I don't believe it,' he growled. 'Sorry about this. I'm not expecting anyone. I'll get rid of whoever it is damned quick.'

As he spoke a smart cream sports car, hood down, rounded the bend in the lane and drew up in a flurry of dust at the gate. Seated at the wheel was a woman with long blonde hair, a flawless, haughty profile, arty sunglasses and an opalescent golden tan.

The sort of tan one gets from winter sports and summer cruises and expensive health clubs, Phoebe thought. She stared in disbelief and froze, her antennae working overtime. No one had to spell it out. She knew that, as unlikely as it seemed, she was looking at the jet-setting raver, Josh's one-time fiancée.

She felt as if she had been punched in the midriff. She exhaled painfully. Of all nights for this to happen. . .when she and Josh. . .this ghost from his past had to turn up. . .it was like a bad dream. . .it couldn't be happening. . .but it was.

Josh snarled an ugly expletive, squared his shoulders and drew himself up to his full, impressive height and grated, 'Brace yourself, love, it's Melanie, my ex-fiancée. I don't know what the bloody hell she's doing here.' He jerked Phoebe savagely to him and put an arm round her waist.

The blonde beauty turned her head and with a slow, leisurely hand took off her sunglasses, revealing cool grey eyes. She curved her lips into a wide, rose-red smile directed at Josh. Phoebe might not have been there. 'Hi, darling,' she drawled. 'Long time no see.'

'Indeed.' His voice was clipped, his face expressionless.

'Too long.' She opened the car door and swung out a pair of endless golden legs and slender bare feet in soft leather sandals and stood up beside the car. She was wand-slim in a body-clinging, shimmering, silk, rose-coloured scrap of a dress that exactly matched her lipstick, her toenails and her tapering fingernails.

She looked sensational as she sauntered across the lane. It suits her—the name, Melanie, thought Phoebe inconsequentionally, struggling to maintain her shattered senses. It sounds rich, soft, spoilt. Her heart dropped like a stone. She'd expected a beauty but not this seductive, languid perfection. No wonder Josh had been— might still be—in love with this gorgeous creature, however much he protested. Few men would be proof against such a fabulously georgeous female.

Panic struck. No way could she compete with that. She felt plain and dowdy in her leafy cotton, ankle-length dress. She must get away.

She tried to free herself from Josh's hold about her waist but he tightened his grasp and pulled her even closer till she was pressed against his side. He was being kind, of course; protective and sensitive to her feelings. It made it all the more unbearable—she couldn't stay and watch him fall prey a second time to the fatal charms of his ex-lover. She glanced up at his face, mutely pleading with him to let her go.

His nostrils were flaring, his mouth a straight line and his eyes like ice. He was very, very angry. Her heart lifted a fraction. She could see no admiration, no longing and no love on his face as he watched Melanie coming towards them. He didn't look like a man besotted.

He didn't sound like it either for he said in

an almost expressionless voice as she reached the gate, 'Hello, Melanie. How are you?' He held out his hand but she tilted up her face for a kiss. Ignoring the mouth which she offered, he bent his head and fleetingly touched a peach-gilded cheek with his lips.

'As you say, it's been a while but I guess in the interim we've both been busy getting on with our lives.' He smiled down at Phoebe and in a plummy, rich, incredibly tender voice murmured, 'Haven't we, my darling?' and dropped a kiss on her head.

Her heart looped the loop and righted itself. He had called her his darling and even if it was partly to impress Melanie she didn't doubt that he had meant it. His face was alight with love. Joy surged through her, leavening the shock of coming face to face with this creature from his past.

She smiled lovingly and intimately up at him and nodded. 'We certainly have.' Then, turning a composed face to Melanie, she held out a steady hand. 'And since Josh seems to have forgotten his manners, let me introduce myself. I'm Phoebe Palmer, a *very* close friend and colleague; and you are. . .?'

Melanie's eyes narrowed and, for a moment, Phoebe thought she was going to ignore her her hand but she didn't. She touched Phoebe's fingers and drawled, 'Melanie Forbes-Wright, and you should know, *Ms* Palmer, that Josh and I are more than close friends.' She slanted a grey eyed glance up at Josh. 'We're. . .'

'Nothing,' Josh ground out savagely. Phoebe felt his muscular body tense against hers. 'We're nothing to each other whatsoever. We were once engaged, disastrously as I remember, but it's over and finished with so stop fantasising, Melanie. Mind your manners and stop being so appallingly rude to Phoebe.' He surveyed her unwaveringly with hard eyes.

There was a silence that seemed to go on endlessly, then a delicate pink flush stained Melanie's cheeks as she stared up at Josh and her arctic grey eyes glittered. 'Don't you dare,' she spat out through stiff lips, 'speak to me like that,' and, raising a slender hand, made to slap his face but he caught and held her wrist.

'Don't even think about it,' he rasped, and dropped her hand, which fell heavily back to her side. 'Now go away, Melanie, you silly woman—and stop making a spectacle of yourself,' he added in a sad voice.

Melanie stared at him for a long moment as all sorts of emotions chased across her face. She opened her mouth as if to speak and then closed it again. Casting Phoebe a look of pure hatred, she said viciously, 'You can have him. He's all yours, the supercilious bastard, but I warn you you'll come second best to his ghastly patients. They're the absolute pits but always first with him.' And, turning on her Italian heels, she picked her way elegantly across the rutted lane to her car.

CHAPTER TEN

JOSH and Phoebe stood side by side, watching in numbed silence as Melanie—rigid with fury—slid behind the steering-wheel. Crashing gears, she did a jerky three-point turn in the narrow lane and sped off, disappearing in a swirl of dust round the bend as thunder rumbled menacingly in the near distance.

They stood there until the sound of the engine died away.

'Exit one poor, mixed-up female,' Josh muttered grimly, sounding more sad than angry. 'I would have done anything to spare you that.' His hand tightened round Phoebe's waist. 'Melanie behaved atrociously towards you, silly, spoilt, impulsive creature that she is. But even for her. . .' he spread his free hand helplessly '. . .it was quite an exhibition. My God, what did she expect? It's been over three bloody years since we parted.'

He drew in a ragged breath and hugged Phoebe still tighter then, nuzzling the top of her head, said in a low, fierce voice, 'It's been one a hell of a shock and I don't know about you, *my darling*, but I could do with a drink.'

His darling again! And said with such force as if he wanted to reassure her and prove to her that Melanie's extraordinary appearance had only served to strengthen his feelings for her, Phoebe. He held her as if afraid of losing her and he had nuzzled the top of her head in such an intimate, possessive, loving manner. She leaned against him, grateful for the solid feel of him as he steered her down the path to the front door.

They stood just inside the door and she was aware of a long, low room, stretching across the width of the cottage, of a beamed ceiling, of white walls, of waxy polish and the scent of flowers. . . She shivered.

'Cold?' he asked softly, pulling her gently round to face him, linking his hands behind her back to keep her close.

She shook her head. 'No, shattered. It's just beginning to hit me. Everything happened so quickly. She appeared and then she disappeared. It was unreal, incredible, that she should turn up like that. And she was so spiteful. Oh, Josh, it was as if she hated me but how could she? She doesn't know me.'

'She recognised you as the other woman, my love—the enemy—but it's me she hates for not welcoming her back with open arms. I should have fallen at her feet and worshipped when she appeared—that's what she expected. She had a hell of a jolt when she saw us together and you know the old saying about a woman scorned. . .'

'But you didn't scorn her originally. She left *you*, didn't she? Broke off your engagement. You were the one who suffered. It was something to do with an accident, wasn't it? At least that's what I heard. . .' She looked up at him, feeling suddenly shy and intrusive. 'Or has the grapevine got it all wrong?'

Josh gave her a long, searching look with sombre, pain-filled eyes, then said quietly, sadly, 'Yes, that's virtually what happened but there was rather more to it than that.' He stroked her cheek and brushed a kiss across her mouth.

'Tell me!' His touch was soothing and electric at the same time. His kiss, light as it was, turned her bones to water and her legs felt as if they were going to give way. She wanted to cling to him but resisted. 'Tell me,' she repeated firmly.

'Are you sure you want to hear? It's not a very edifying story. I don't want to bore you.'

He dropped his hands from her face and she stepped back from him. 'Don't be ridiculous. You know you couldn't do that. I want to know all there is to know about you. You invited me here to talk, Josh, so let's talk.' She felt all at once detached, determined to learn the truth about his past and what made this man—with whom she had fallen so deeply and utterly in love in such a short time—tick. Somehow, Melanie's whirlwind visit made it terribly important that she do so.

He produced a quirky, lopsided smile but he looked strained and his eyes were bleak. 'You're a hard woman, Phoebe Palmer. But, OK, I'll talk and then it'll be your turn to do the same, just as we promised each other last night.' Then, suddenly brisk, he said, 'But I invited you not only to talk but to supper. Wouldn't you like to eat first?'

She shook her head. 'Couldn't. Not yet. Food would choke me.'

'No matter. It'll keep—it's just soup and a

ham salad and fruit. I'm no Gary Rhodes in the kitchen. Now come and sit down.'

He took her hand and drew her across the room to where a comfortable-looking sofa and three chunky armchairs, linen-covered in muted autumnal shades of green and brown and orange, were grouped cosily round a brick inglenook fireplace filled with neatly hewn logs. Brass fire-irons and a full, brass wood box gleamed in the hearth.

Somewhat overwhelmed by its cosy perfection, she sank down into one of the armchairs.

'Do make yourself at home,' he said, 'while I get our drinks. What would you like—sherry, whiskey, brandy, gin?' He smiled down at her and the smile reached his eyes, wiping out the bleakness. It was clear that he wanted only to please her.

His warm, intimate, loving manner was reassuring. 'A gin with lots of ice and tonic would be nice.'

'Right, coming up. I keep the drinks in the kitchen. Won't be a minute.' He disappeared through an archway beneath the open-tread wooden stairs.

After a moment she found herself relaxing a

little and gazed round the rest of the room with interest. Josh's room, in his cottage which he jealously guarded and called his bolt-hole, where friends normally called by invitation only. Except, she thought wryly, for the Melanies of this world with their brash, brittle sophistication. She was conscious that she was a privileged invited guest because Josh had wanted her there.

It was a very long room with wide casement windows at either end and along the west-facing wall looking out over the front garden. It was not as formally austere or aggressively masculine as she had thought it might be, but homely; and somewhere along the line there was a woman's touch. A housekeeper, a daily treasure?

There were heavy-weave, mushroom-coloured curtains at the windows and crammed bookcases beneath—a colourful jumble of leather-bound editions and paperbacks. Brilliant, jewel-like rugs were scattered over the dark, polished parquet floor and several fine flower studies hung on the plain cream walls.

A bowl of glowing orange and yellow marigolds and nasturtiums graced a low occasional table just inside the front door. The far end of the room was obviously the dining area where an elegant oval table, ringed with high-backed tapestry-covered chairs, stood ready laid for a meal. There were flowers on the table, a low arrangement of roses and ferns.

A thrill of pleasure swept through her, swamping the unpleasant memory of Melanie's visit—what a lot of trouble Josh had gone to to make her feel welcome.

She smiled inwardly, savouring the thought, and at that moment he reappeared with their drinks, ducking his head as he came through the archway. He handed her a tall, slim glass clinking with ice.

'It's a lovely room,' Phoebe said, waving a hand. 'Not a bit what I expected.'

'What did you expect?'

'Something much more masculine, more austere, lots of heavy leather. Not the flowers. I suppose you've got someone who comes in and cleans? Everything's so beautifully polished and cared for.'

He grinned. 'And a mere man's not capable of that?'

Phoebe shook her head. 'I didn't say that.

You've not got the time—you spend so much with your patients.'

'You're dead right, I haven't. Emmy Foster, the gardener's wife, comes in each day and keeps things ticking over. Spoils me. But the flower arrangements are mine. It's my hobby—my garden and old-fashioned flowers. Great therapy, gardening, though city girl that you are I suppose you don't know much about it, do you?'

He stood in front of the fireplace, legs slightly apart in a very male stance, looking down at her and smiling faintly. 'But perhaps that can be remedied in the near future.'

Was he playing for time? He was way off-beam if he thought that he was going to sidetrack her into a discussion about gardening. She looked down into her glass and swirled the clear liquid around, took a sip and said abruptly, 'Josh, tell me about you and Melanie. I want to know what happened—why she left you after your accident when you must have most needed her.'

Josh stopped smiling, nodded and lowered himself into an armchair, beside her and partly facing her. 'Yes, of course you want to know and I owe you that.' He took a swig of whiskey and said flatly, 'She couldn't stand the scars. That's finally why she left me, though things had been. . .'

Phoebe interrupted sharply, 'Scars, what scars?'

Josh shrugged. 'On my face—chin mostly, hence the beard.' He rubbed his hand round his jaw. 'And broken glass made a mess of my back and one leg was smashed up—still makes me limp sometimes due to weather or stress. And I had a laminectomy to relieve pressure on the spinal column, which had been damaged in the accident. It was a neat surgical scar yet, for some reason, Melanie hated that more than anything.'

'Do you mean to say that she left you because of a few scars—the woman who was engaged to you and was supposed to be in love with you?' Phoebe stared at him with shocked soft brown eyes. 'Oh, Josh, I'm so sorry. It must have hurt you dreadfully.' She put out her hand and laid it for a moment on his arm.

He said quietly, 'Yes it did at first, like hell, even though things were already becoming unstuck between us. But Melanie doesn't understand illness or disfigurement. Anything short of physical perfection appalls her. Well, you've seen her—she's flawless and looks for flawlessness in others.'

He paused and gulped down a mouthful of whiskey. 'But it wasn't just that I was suddenly not the perfect specimen that parted us—that was just the final straw. We didn't see eye to eye on my career in medicine.

'When we met I was specialising in neurosurgery, a registrar with Professor Pickering's firm. She saw me as a successful consultant with a private practice. I planned to work for the health service, attached to one of the teaching hospitals doing research. Things would never have worked out between us. We were poles apart in our thinking.'

Phoebe didn't answer at once but took another sip of her drink and stared unseeingly down into its depths as her thoughts raced.

She doubted if Melanie was capable of doing much constructive thinking. Everything about her screamed empty-headed bimbo. But a beautiful bimbo, capable of turning any man's head, however intelligent he might be, if she set what little mind she had to it. Even level-headed Josh would have found it hard to resist.

And Josh would have been worth pursuing—wealthy in his own right, a member of an old county family, a brilliant, handsome surgeon working for a distinguished consultant, superficially a perfect match. It was easy to see how a rich, impressionable young woman might have been attracted to, even fancied herself in love with, such a successful man and singled him out for her attention.

But had Josh ever been in love with her or had he simply been infatuated? Did it matter? Hadn't he had made it abundantly clear that things had begun to fall apart from the time she had come between him and his work? Medicine was his first love, his true love.

But why had he given up surgery in favour of the much less glamorous field of post-trauma control and convalescent patients? Because of the accident? Had that been responsible for his change of career course?

As she opened her mouth to ask a huge clap of thunder cracked overhead and a sheet of lightning lit up the room. Large, fat raindrops began spattering against the open windows and Josh, with a murmured apology, stood up and, crossing the broad expanse of the polished floor, began closing them one by one down the length of the room.

'Jolly good job,' he said as, limping slightly, he walked back from the dining end of the long, low beamed room, 'that I closed the upstairs windows earlier before I went into the garden.'

He was silhouetted against the brassy light seeping through the latticed windows, his tawny mane of hair glowing gold. He looked magnificent and, in spite of the limp, strong and invincible.

Phoebe's heart missed several beats and seemed to swell in her chest and her breasts rose and fell rapidly as she watched him coming toward her. Time froze. She ached, longed, to feel his arms about her. Nothing else mattered. Whether he had been in love with the beautiful Melanie or why he had given up surgery didn't matter. She just wanted him to tell her that it was *her* he now loved and this time she would believe him.

She felt light-headed, faint with relief.

With an unsteady hand she placed her glass on the low oak table beside her chair and rose slowly to her feet. He was only a yard from her now. His brilliant blue eyes swept over her upturned face and met her own soft brown, gold-flecked eyes unswervingly and read the message of love in them. He held out his arms and mutely she stepped forward into them and he wrapped them round her, crushing her against his chest.

There was no need for words. They stood locked together for long moments, his face buried in her bob of glossy brown hair. They didn't speak or even kiss at first but were content to be close moulded against each other, his hardness thrusting into her soft yielding body as his hands cupped her neat buttocks and pressed her to him.

Phoebe could hear and feel the strong, steady beat of his heart through the thin silk of his open-necked shirt and she was conscious of the fuzz of tawny blond hair trailing down from his throat. She nuzzled against the V of his shirt with teeth and lips, forcing another button open, nibbling, tugging none too gently at the short curly hairs until he muttered a muffled expletive and pulled fractionally away from her.

She lifted her head and smiled up at him and on a long, drawn-out sigh murmured, 'I've wanted to do that for ages.'

His eyes, almost violet, blazed down at her.

'And I've been wanting to do this,' he rasped, and brought his mouth down hard on hers, forcing her lips and then her teeth apart with the tip of his long, strong, probing tongue.

A tide of ecstasy flooded through her and with wild abandon she responded, sliding her own tongue over his, exploring his mouth as he explored hers. She linked her hands behind his muscled neck and pushed and tangled her fingers in his thick mane of hair. She felt exultant, free.

Through the thin cotton of her dress she could feel his hands moving rhythmically up and down her spine from taut buttocks to quivering ribcage as his thumbs kneaded the soft flesh beneath her armpits where the swell of her breasts began. And the hardness of his arousal thrust and pulsed against her soft, sensitive vulva.

She shuddered violently as he rubbed rhythmically against her until she felt a moistness between her thighs as her longing to feel him inside her spiralled almost beyond control.

Josh made a guttural sound in his throat and pulled his mouth from hers but his rock-hard column continued to thrust against her, demanding and possessive.

He growled thickly, 'I love you and I want you, Phoebe, but only if you want me too.' His eyes were wide and dark, glowing with desire.

'You know that I do,' she whispered through bruised lips.

'But not here,' he said. 'Upstairs, properly, in the bedroom.' And before she could protest he'd swept her up in his arms and was striding toward the open staircase.

'Put me down,' she begged as they reached the first stair. 'Your back, your leg!'

He gave a bark of boyish, unrestrained laughter. 'To hell with my leg. I could climb a mountain with you in my arms,' he cried joyfully, cradling her against his broad muscular chest. 'You're like a feather, my darling.'

Phoebe felt his vibrant, exuberant strength surging through him and reaching out to her. Here was the tough warrior Viking of her dream, not the cool, reserved doctor with whom she worked daily. This other passionate man whom she alone was privileged to see. A thousand butterflies seemed to flutter in her abdomen and she ached between her thighs.

He reached the top of the stairs and crossed a spacious landing to a white-painted door that stood ajar. He pushed it open with his foot. 'My room,' he said, then with a throaty laugh, 'No, *our* room from now on.'

Phoebe lifted her head from his chest and gazed round. She had an impression of a large, light, white airy room with sloping ceilings and overhanging eaves of thatch visible through the rain-splashed latticed windows; of pale curtains and carpet and a large shadowy desk, with keyboard and screen, beneath one window.

Against the centre of the long wall, facing the windows, was an enormous, antique, shining brass bedstead draped with an exquisite patchwork coverlet, all blues and golds and reds. The whole effect was bold and magnificent and handsome. Just like Josh, thought Phoebe, with his blue eyes and shock of bright hair.

She said breathlessly, 'It's a beautiful room, so right for you. Perfect,' and murmured with a shy, dimpling smile, 'And the bed is georgeous—it's vast.'

'There's rather a lot of me to accommodate,' he replied with an answering smile and added in a low murmur, 'But, even so, there's room enough for two.' He bent his head to trail a lingering kiss across her forehead.

She was suddenly sharply aware of many small things. His breath fanning her face, the faint sharp sweet scent of expensive soap emanating from his warm skin as his bearded chin brushed her cheek, of his eyes dark and hypnotic meeting hers; of thunder rumbling around, flashes of lightning, rain pelting at the windows.

Grave, violet-blue eyes, full of hunger and desire, continued to hold hers as he lowered her gently onto the bed. He said huskily, 'I've waited for this moment for weeks that have seemed like years, my darling Phoebe, but I want you to want me as much as I want you and love you.'

'But you must know that I do,' she whispered, stretching out a hand and rubbing gently at his beard—the beard that she had once hated and that she now found sexy and sophisticated and so right.

To her surprise, instead of lying on the bed with her, he knelt down beside it, rolled her onto her side facing him, caught both her hands between his and said in a low, firm voice, 'But before we make love, which I long to do, dear, sweet Phoebe, I want you to see me naked, scars and all. I know you're not squeamish but my back's not a pretty sight. I don't want to hide anything from you. There musn't be any hang-ups for either of us.'

His words were totally unexpected and Phoebe couldn't answer at once. All sorts of emotions raged through her. How could he break the magic of the wonderful vibes that were flowing between them and wipe away the last few glorious, passionate minutes? Anger welled up and suffused her. How could he think that her love was so shallow as to care about a few, or even many, scars?

She was shaken to the core.

He still held her hands captive but she struggled up onto one elbow and thrust her face, eyes blazing, close to his and spat out, 'Do you really think that my love is such a poor thing that it can be turned off by a few scars? I'm not your precious rich bitch, Melanie. I'm a normal, healthy woman and I'm a nurse, Josh, in case you've forgotten. I'm used to dealing with dis-figurement in all its guises.

'Physical perfection is only skin-deep. You, above all people, should know that. My God, you preach it to your patients often enough.'

Josh freed her hands and with long fingers smoothed back a few stray hairs from her angry face. He looked steadily into her eyes. 'And it's true but I had to ask, dear love,' he murmured. 'I had to hear you say that you love me enough to accept me as I am—that the scars don't matter,' and, barely audibly, added, 'You see, Melanie made me feel a freak and at times I still do. I know I shouldn't but I do.'

He continued to look at her steadily, his eyes not giving anything away, but a rueful smile touched his mouth and in a voice full of bitter irony he said, 'You'd be quite entitled to say, ''physician heal thyself.''' He shrugged eloquently.

'And I should be able to but I can't, not without support. You see, the accident was a bad one. A child died, a driver was brain-damaged and survives like a zombie. And I was trapped, in a pretty bad way myself, not able to do anything. God, I felt guilty as hell. Will you give me that support, Phoebe, help me to overcome the physical and emotional scars?'

He raised his leonine head proudly, asking but not pleading, his eyes never leaving hers.

She felt her anger slip away, submerged in an overwhelming tidal wave of love for this man who was the rock on which she and so many depended. And the accident and its aftermath explained much, not least why he was able to understand trauma and counsel so wisely and yet could not come to terms with his own condition. That he asked for her help was not a sign of weakness but of strength. Only a morally strong man would admit to needing help.

'You know that I will, Josh,' she said simply. She swung herself round until she was sitting on the edge of the bed, her legs straddling his kneeling figure, her hands on his powerful shoulders. 'But we'll undress together—reveal ourselves to each other as lovers should, naked and unashamed.'

Josh opened his mouth to say something but Phoebe placed a finger over his lips. 'It's the best way, dearest love,' she murmured, not even noticing the endearment that came so naturally to her. 'I've got scars, too. Oh, not ones that you can see but hurts from the past. I had a relationship that went badly wrong. I'm scared that I might fail you.'

To her utter astonishment and shame, tears

that she couldn't hold back welled up and trickled down her cheeks. She leaned forward and rested her forehead against his. He wrapped his arms about her and stood up, taking her with him, and showered kisses on her wet cheeks and eyelids.

'I'm so sorry,' she wailed. 'I'm supposed to be supporting you and look at me, leaning on you like I always do—like everyone does. What the hell must you think of me?'

Josh tilted her back her head and looked down into her tear-drenched eyes. '*I think*,' he said slowly, 'that you are the best thing that ever happened to me. I think that you are warm and beautiful and loving and that I want to marry you and cherish you for ever.'

'*Marry me*? But I thought. . .' She sought for the right words. 'A loving friendship, a relation-ship. You don't have to marry me. I'm not into one-night stands but. . .'

'Are you against marriage or afraid of it, Phoebe, on account of your own and your mother's rotten experience?'

She shook her head and smiled tremulously. 'No, I don't think so, not if it's to the right man.'

'Well, I'm the right man and an old-fashioned

man, my love. I don't want a relationship, however committed. That may suit some people but not me. I want the world to know that we belong to each other for keeps.'

He pressed her closer until her breasts were crushed against his chest and again she could feel the hard thrust of him against her own pulsing softness. He bent his head and kissed her cheeks, her eyelids, her slender throat and, finally, with great tenderness, lingeringly, her mouth. The passion was still there but subdued.

With equal tenderness Phoebe returned his kiss. As she kissed him she slipped her hands round his waist, eased his shirt free of his trousers and, with great gentleness, began exploring his broad back.

Josh stiffened for a moment and then relaxed. 'So be it,' he said.

His back was for the most part smooth but she occasionally detected a small indent or raised area, denoting old scar tissue or a plastic repair and, as expected, his laminectomy scar. Lovingly she ran her fingers down the long, neat, vertical indent beside his spine and murmured softly, 'I love you, Dr Richmond, scars and all, and I'll take you up on that offer of marriage if you will take me on the same terms.'

'I will take you on any terms,' said Josh with a smile so brilliant that it made her heart turn over. 'As long as we can be together always as friends and lovers.'

'As friends and lovers,' repeated Phoebe and, without feeling the least self-conscious, added, 'till death us do part.' Her eyes, fixed on his, were huge and lustrous and full of longing. 'Now, please, Josh, make love to me,' she begged.

They were married six weeks later in the packed village church.

Phoebe wore an oyster satin gown, very simple, with a scooped-out neckline filled with a double string of lustrous pearls, a family heirloom that Josh had given her for a wedding present.

The Laird of Malt, Lady Richmond's brother, who had returned with her from Scotland a month earlier, gave Phoebe away; and Maeve, striking in a peony-pink frothy dress, which contrasted brilliantly with her red hair, was her bridesmaid.

Josh's elder brother, Laurie, tore himself

away from his South American dig to be his best man.

During the service Lady Richmond, beautifully elegant, sat in the front pew on the bridegroom's side of the aisle, with the Scottish clan Malt gathered behind her.

'But,' she whispered to Phoebe, kissing her warmly on both cheeks as they lined up for a photographic session outside the church, 'though I was sitting on my grandson's side of the aisle I consider myself *in loco parentis* to both of you. I'm your granny as well as Josh's—never forget that—and my family is your family.'

'I won't,' promised Phoebe, and blinked back the tears as she smiled tremulously up at Josh standing beside her, large and handsome, magnificent in his clan kilt, his mane of tawny hair gleaming in the sunshine.

With his Celtic intuition he homed in at once why her eyes were glistening with unshed tears and said softly, 'Your mother would be happy for you today, my darling. She and Granny would have hit it off famously. And she would be so happy to know that you have gained a granny as well as a husband who will care for you and cherish you always.'

Phoebe swallowed her tears. 'Yes, I know she would,' she whispered, and, feeling wrapped round by his love and comforted by him as always, turned to smile at the camera.

MEDICAL ROMANCE™

Large Print

Titles for the next six months...

June

RESPONDING TO TREATMENT	Abigail Gordon
BRIDAL REMEDY	Marion Lennox
A WISH FOR CHRISTMAS	Josie Metcalfe
WINGS OF DUTY	Meredith Webber

July

TAKE A CHANCE ON LOVE	Jean Evans
PARTNERS IN LOVE	Maggie Kingsley
DRASTIC MEASURES	Laura MacDonald
PERFECT PARTNERS	Carol Wood

August

IF YOU NEED ME...	Caroline Anderson
A SURGEON TO TRUST	Janet Ferguson
VALENTINE'S HUSBAND	Josie Metcalfe
WINGS OF PASSION	Meredith Webber

MEDICAL ROMANCE™

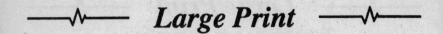 *Large Print*

MEDICAL ROMANCE™

—⋀— Large Print —